THE
BILLIONAIRE'S
BABY

THE BILLIONAIRE'S BABY

BY

NICOLA MARSH

First published in Great Britain 2009
Large Print edition 2009
Harlequin Mills & Boon Limited,
Eton House, 18-24 Paradise Road,
Richmond, Surrey TW9 1SR

© Nicola Marsh 2009   ∫00982501

ISBN: 978 0 263 20624 1

Set in Times Roman 16½ on 18½ pt.
16-0909-48803

Harlequin Mills & Boon policy is to use papers that are
natural, renewable and recyclable products and made
from wood grown in sustainable forests. The logging and
manufacturing process conform to the legal environmental
regulations of the country of origin.

Printed and bound in Great Britain
by CPI Antony Rowe, Chippenham, Wiltshire

*For my fab editor, Lucy, who went above and beyond
the call of duty with this one. Thanks, Lucy!*

CHAPTER ONE

CAMRYN HENDERSON hated Valentine's Day.

A day designed to highlight over-the-top, mushy commercialism. All that hearts-and-flowers claptrap might work for those foolish enough to believe in romance, but she knew better.

Boy, did she know better.

'That was some turnout today, huh?'

Camryn stopped swiping at the immaculate stainless-steel surface behind the bar and mustered a tired smile for Anna, her best employee and closest friend.

'Our biggest day all year.'

She propped against the bar and shifted her weight from one aching foot to the other. Her favourite knee-high black leather boots with a two-inch block heel might look great and add to her street cred as a hip young thing running the trendiest café in Melbourne's Docklands, but built for comfort they weren't.

'Every café and restaurant along this stretch was packed today. Nice to know romance is alive and well.'

Camryn refrained from wrinkling her nose in disgust at the mention of romance—just.

'Sure, it's great for business but, personally, I think it's a bit lame. All pomp and show for one day when for the rest of the year those couples probably barely speak to each other.'

She'd worked Valentine's Day for the last six years, forced to watch cosy couples mooning over each other, the intimate smiles, the hand-holding, the roses, even the occasional marriage proposal.

She'd seen it all, had been relieved to have distanced herself from all that fanciful nonsense, but it was times like now, when the café had all but emptied and the tea candles had burned low, that she couldn't help but wish for something she'd once had on this day…a lifetime ago.

'You're the only woman I know who doesn't have a romantic bone in her body.' Anna waved a finger in front of her face and tut-tutted.

'Maybe you should let the little fat guy with the bow fire an arrow your way for once.'

'Not on your life.'

She'd already been stung in the butt by one of Cupid's arrows and had the scars to prove it.

'Besides, I've found my niche.'

They laughed as she picked up a black serviette with a bold fuchsia *Café Niche* printed on it and thrust it towards Anna. 'See, it says so right here.'

'And what the boss says goes. Yeah, yeah, I know.' Anna shook her head. 'Well, want to know what I think?'

Camryn grinned as she poured milk into a stainless-steel jug, hankering for a frothy cappuccino before wrapping things up for the night. 'You're going to tell me anyway, so go ahead.'

Anna smirked as she slid two cups onto saucers and readied the espresso machine.

'I think Cupid likes a challenge, and you, my friend, are it. The ultimate romantic rebel. Wouldn't it be a notch in his bow to get you all hot and bothered over some guy?'

'Sooo not going to happen.'

Her mouth twitched. If her friend only knew how hot and bothered she'd once been over a guy and what had happened on this particular day. 'Though I kind of like the thought of being a rebel. Makes me want to wear black leather to work.'

Anna raised an eyebrow and sent a pointed look at her boots. 'You already do.'

She grimaced as she wiggled a foot. 'Yeah, and it's killing me.'

'You don't get to look as good as we do without a little pain.'

Anna cinched her belt, made entirely of interlocking silver circles, tighter around her ample waist and patted what she proudly referred to as her 'bountiful booty'. 'Besides, wish I could get away with wearing what you do. However, skinny jeans, clingy silk tops and knee-high boots just aren't me.'

'You always look great,' Camryn said, silently agreeing the typical outfit she wore to work definitely wouldn't flatter her vertically challenged, curvaceous friend.

'Thanks, hon. Now, let me make the cappuccinos while you hustle the last stragglers out the door.'

Anna jerked her head in the direction of a table near the floor-to-ceiling glass windows over-looking the spectacular Melbourne city night skyline. 'It isn't as if they're here waiting for Cupid to strike.'

Camryn laughed as she glanced over at the two tradesmen, Dirk and Mike, who religiously fre-quented the café, poring over house plans spread across the table.

'Hey, you never know. Maybe they're planning on building their dream home?'

Anna quirked an eyebrow as both heads turned in sync as a blonde in a mini skirt walked past outside. 'Uh, I don't think so. Now, shoo! Give them a delicate shove out the door so we can put our feet up and get a decent caffeine hit before we lock up.'

'Actually, the guys have organised a project manager to meet me here tonight to discuss the renovations on my apartment, so I'll have to wait around till he arrives. Why don't we skip the coffee and you head home? I'll lock up.'

'Sure thing, boss.' Anna sent her a mock salute and grinned. 'Want me to turn down the lights to discourage other customers from dropping in? And flick the sign on the door?'

'I'll do it. Thanks, have a good night.'

As Camryn walked the length of the bar to the power box, she glanced at her watch, hoping the project manager would arrive soon. She needed the renovations done asap, and all the other builders she'd tried had fobbed her off with 'I'm too busy' lines or tried to rip her off because she was a woman.

And she hated that. She hadn't got where she was today without being strong and independent and focused on her goals, something chauvinistic guys just didn't understand.

Flicking two switches to dim the lights, she had her finger poised over a third when a man pushed through the front door.

'Great. He's finally here,' she thought as she flicked the last switch and picked up the set of hefty keys to lock up, eager to get this meeting underway.

However, as she neared the door, the keys

crashed to the floor, along with her hopes for a productive consultation, her heart stopping when she got a closer look at the man who'd just entered.

Scruffy, wind-tossed, ultra casual.

Faded denim, soft grey T-shirt, worn leather work boots.

Stubble shadows, laugh-lines around grey eyes, slight dimples bracketing a mouth made for smiling.

A mouth that was smiling at her, a wide, genuine smile filled with warmth, a smile that packed a punch, a smile she could never forget no matter how hard she tried.

And she'd tried. She'd tried for six long, lonely years, yet the minute Blane Andrews strolled in and smiled that all-too-familiar smile, she was instantly transported back in time.

To the first time she'd seen that smile, on Valentine's Day, as fate would have it, to a time when that smile rarely left his face, when he'd lavished her with attention, when they'd been crazy for each other.

Seeing him again after all these years was like being sucked into a vortex of swirling memories of love and laughter and sunshine on a hot summer's day beside a lazy, meandering creek.

Of sharing hot dogs perched on the back of his rusty old Ford, watching the sun set, wiping ketchup off each other with smiles on their faces and love in their hearts.

Of taking long slow walks hand in hand in the shade of towering eucalypts, oblivious to the bush beauty, focused solely on each other.

Of cuddling and kissing and floating on air, lost in the exquisite, heady perfection of first love.

Oh, yeah, falling for Blane had been a whirlwind of exhilarating highs, before being spit out the other side, left with nothing but pain and loss and devastation.

He'd ripped her heart out, and she never wanted to feel that way again.

Ever.

'Everything okay, Cam?'

'You mean right now or are you asking how I've been the last six years?'

Trying not to show how rattled she was by his reappearance and the abbreviated form of her name only he had ever called her, she bent to pick up the keys at the same time he did, their fingers brushing, hers tingling, his long and warm and heartrendingly familiar.

She jerked back, straightening too quickly, and his hand shot out to steady her elbow, the barest of touches enough to give her dormant hormones a jolt.

'Both.'

He scanned her face as if looking for answers, those slate-grey eyes as frank and warm as they'd always been, beautiful, honest eyes that said trust me.

Foolishly, she'd once complied.

'I'm fine.'

A big, fat lie if ever she heard one. How could she be fine when the love of her life, the man who'd walked out on her without an explanation, came waltzing in here on the anniversary of the day she'd first handed him her heart? Only to have it carved up three months later.

'What are you doing here?' she blurted, sliding the key ring from index finger to index finger, the jangle as the keys clinked and clanked against one another deafening in the growing silence.

'I came to see you.'

Her heart thudded at the sincerity in his eyes.

He was telling the truth.

She may not have seen him for six years but she'd never forget the way she could always read his moods by the blue flecks in his eyes.

Indigo indicated happiness—the kind of intense, spontaneous happiness they'd had for twelve all-too-brief weeks.

Cobalt indicated honesty—she'd believed him when he'd said she was the only girl for him, that they'd always be together, that he'd love her for ever.

Deep smoky-gentian meant passion—the mind-blowing, unforgettable, once-in-a-lifetime connection they'd shared.

Oh, yeah, she could remember each and every shade of those flecks, had lost herself in those grey depths for three blissful months. Until he'd walked away.

So what if those flecks glowed cobalt now? Did his honesty count for anything when he hadn't been able to face her with the truth before leaving?

Hating the surge of emotion making her

tummy gripe, she stepped back, forcing him to release his hold on her elbow and instantly missing the contact.

Irrational, stupid and crazy, but her body had softened under his touch, had leaned towards him, recognising on some subconscious level the one guy to ever know her intimately. And by the strange heat seeping through her muscles, her traitorous body was rejoicing despite the hard-learned lesson that he couldn't be trusted.

'You came to see me? Well, here I am. Now that you've seen me, why don't you leave?'

He smiled, and she struggled not to gasp at the impact, her pulse doing a familiar tango through her veins.

'You can't get rid of me that easily.'

'Could've fooled me,' she snapped, mentally clapping one hand over her mouth while slapping herself upside the head with the other.

An emotional outburst like that would suggest she still cared—which she didn't, she couldn't—and the last thing she needed was him hanging around trying to rehash the past.

To her chagrin he laughed, a rich, natural

sound that warmed her better than any cappuccino she'd ever drunk. And she'd drunk the equivalent of a year's supply of Brazil beans after he'd left, to recapture half the heat he used to make her feel.

'Guess I deserved that.'

'And the rest.'

The laugh-lines around his eyes deepened. 'Go ahead. Get it all out of your system.'

'Don't tempt me.'

She toyed with the keys, torn between the urge to take him up on his offer and tell him how heartbroken she'd been, how she'd searched for him for a year, how she hadn't let another guy close because of him and the emotional fallout from their intense relationship—and booting him out the door and never giving him another thought.

'Cam, I know you don't want to kick me out.'

Great, he could still read her mind, could hone in on how she was feeling, and there was something about the way he looked at her, as if he could see right down to her soul and knew better than she did that the last thing she wanted to do was kick him out.

For as much as she wanted him to walk right back out that door and never come back—he was good at that—a huge part of her clamoured to know where he'd been, what he'd been doing and why he'd ripped their perfect world apart.

'You don't know what I want anymore,' she said, hating the flare of hurt in his eyes and how much her heart ached in response.

'I'd like to.'

His intent was clear, and she inhaled sharply, his poignantly familiar, fresh outdoorsy scent reminiscent of crushed cedar leaves in a spring shower, the tantalising trace filling her nose, her lungs, making her want to lean into the soft, sensitive spot under his jaw and nuzzle him as she used to.

Ignoring the incredible yearning to do just that, she rattled the keys.

'I'm closing up.'

He raised an eyebrow and glanced at the lights she'd dimmed. 'I can see that, but we really need to talk.'

'Actually, we don't.'

Because if she let him talk, let him explain why he'd run out on her all those years ago, she'd be compelled to relive the pain, and there was no way she'd go through that heart-break again.

She'd built a new life in the years since he'd split, a better life, an independent life where she didn't need anything or anyone, and she'd like to keep it that way.

Leaning forward, he touched her cheek, the calluses on his finger-pads rasping against her skin and sending a tiny shiver of longing through her.

She remembered all too well how those work-roughened hands felt caressing her body, how gentle yet arousing they could be. How they used to circle her waist, lift her up and spin her around till she was dizzy with the motion and the sheer joy of being with him. How strong and sure they'd been, stroking her that very first time, initiating her into pleasures she'd only ever dreamed about.

'I won't take no for an answer.'

His fingertips lingered an exquisite moment longer before he dropped his hand.

Shaking her head, she bit back the urge to laugh. There was nothing remotely funny about having the man she'd once loved badger her after all this time, but the young, impulsive guy she'd known back then had never been this determined, this stubborn.

'One coffee then you're out of here. Take it or leave it.'

'I'll take it.'

'Fine. Choose your poison and make it snappy.'

He grinned as he rocked back on his heels, hands thrust into pockets, confident he'd wear her down.

As if.

'You sure have a way with customers.'

'You're not a customer, you're my…' She trailed off, not wanting to go there. She'd shut the door on the past, why open it and risk the future she'd worked so hard to build?

'Go on, say it. I'm your?'

'You know,' she bit out, sending him a withering glare that made little impact if his widening grin was any indication. 'You better order that coffee before I renege and bundle you out of here right this very minute.'

He chuckled, and rather than it riling her, she could barely clamp down on the urge to join in.

He'd always done this: made her laugh, made

her see the lighter side of any situation—a genuine glass-half-full kind of guy. She'd loved that about him. She'd loved many things about him, which had made it all the harder to get over him.

Gritting her teeth, she prompted again, 'Coffee?'

'The usual, please.'

'Coming right up.'

She swivelled on her heel, realising her mistake a second too late. Now he'd know she remembered how he preferred his coffee. Not a great start to showing him how she'd got over him.

The gentle hand on her shoulder pulled her up, her body's reaction to his innocuous touch totally flummoxing.

'Cam, I just want to say hello to some guys I know, and I'll be back in a moment.'

Amusement sparked in the depths of his grey eyes, as if he were privy to some private joke, before he dropped his hand and turned away, leaving her flustered, confused and staring at a very fine butt.

Hearing him call her Cam resurrected memories of the way he'd breezed into Rainbow Creek one sunny Saturday morning, strolled into her parents' coffee shop, took one look at her name badge and said, 'I'll have an espresso, please, Cam' with a twinkle in his eye and a smile on his boyish face.

She'd been a goner, instantly falling head over heels for the laid-back, nomadic builder who'd taken a piece of her heart along with a huge chunk of her pride when he'd left.

As for that butt...tight, firm, filling out the seat of his worn denim very nicely, thank you very much...oh, no, she wouldn't dwell on how long it had been since she'd admired it, gripped it...

'No, no, no,' she muttered, grabbing the end of her French braid and fiddling with the elastic, hoping her plait hadn't unravelled along with her common sense.

Valentine's Day had really got to her, and, calling the chubby cherub some rather nasty names under her breath, she marched across the café and slid behind the bar.

One espresso, extra-strong, two sugars, and laid-back Blane with the twinkly eyes and charming smile could take his sexy butt and hightail it out of here, leaving her to do what she did best: run the best damn café in Melbourne.

'Hey, how're the plans coming along?'

Blane slid into a chair next to the two guys who were helping him turn his dream into a reality.

An adjunct to his dream, he thought, as his glance flicked to the bar, drawn to the sassy brunette paying an inordinate amount of attention to the espresso machine.

She'd changed so much.

Her short spikes had gone, replaced by a long plait hanging halfway down her back, the three ear studs were down to one, and the lean body he remembered all too well had morphed into curves. Eye-catching, gorgeous curves he couldn't take his eyes off.

Though the biggest change was her personality. Gone was the impressionable, spontaneous girl he'd known and loved and in her place, a blunt, confident woman who had no qualms about declaring how unwelcome he was.

Not that he expected any less. For what he'd put them both through he deserved it.

But there hadn't been a choice, and, glancing around the café, her dream a reality, and back to her deftly making his coffee just the way he liked it, he knew he'd done the right thing.

Besides, she might act as if he was as welcome as a cockroach at her café, but there'd been something about the way her brown eyes had sparked when she'd seen him, the way she'd reacted to his touch…it had given him hope.

'See for yourself.' Dirk, the cabinetmaker, pushed the plans across to him. 'The architect's made changes to the guest bedrooms, as you requested, and we've run with the new specifications. What do you think?'

He studied the tiny straight lines, the numbered annotations, and ruffled the hair at his nape, a habit he'd acquired while labouring over countless financial reports during the years it had taken BA Constructions to become a rival of the biggest guns in Australia's building industry.

'Looks okay to me.'

The pungent aroma of freshly brewed coffee, strong and bittersweet, drew his attention away from the plans and back to the bar where Cam was placing a steaming cup on a saucer.

He studied her with the same focus he'd shown for the plans, noting the tendrils escaping her plait, curling in defiance around her heart-shaped face, the high cheekbones, the mouth a tad on the full side to be strictly beautiful.

His gaze drifted lower to a funky, bright top whose colour defied logic but blended perfectly with the colour scheme of the place—all bright pinks and blues and golds—to the hint of cleavage which resurrected memories of how she'd felt in his hands, the sounds she'd made the first time he'd touched her…

A short, shrill whistle interrupted his journey down erotic lane, and his gaze snapped up to meet hers—questioning, daring, challenging, as if she'd caught him checking her out and was calling him on it—as she crooked a finger at him and pointed to the steaming espresso on the bar.

'I told you Cam's great. Serves the best coffee this side of the Yarra. Mike and I always come here for meetings.'

'So you said.'

Blane couldn't thank Dirk enough for letting slip this vital bit of information when he'd arrived in Melbourne a week ago. He'd barely begun his search for her when he'd found her, and, now that he had, he had no intention of letting her slip away.

As for the guys telling him she needed a project manager for renovations on her apartment, it had been a stroke of pure luck.

He'd been hell-bent on barging in here the minute he'd discovered her whereabouts, but once he'd discovered that particular titbit of information, he'd bided his time over the week, knowing she'd be more responsive to him on a professional rather than personal level.

Not that he intended to keep the status quo that way for long.

'Back in a sec.'

Pushing his chair back, he headed for the bar, deliberately slowing his stride when in fact he felt like sprinting. In all honesty, if she whistled and crooked her finger at him again with that 'come and get it' look in her eye, he'd probably do a mean pole-vaulting impression over the bar, too.

'Here you go. One extra-snappy espresso.'

She pushed the cup towards him, the saucer sliding across the squeaky-clean steel bar.

'You only made it snappy so you can get rid of me.'

Her wry smile did little to detract from the cheeky gleam in her eyes. 'Well, looks like you haven't lost your mind-reading abilities.'

'I guess not. Care to test me out?'

She shook her head and laughed, the familiar low chuckles sending warmth spiralling through him. 'Trust me, you don't want to know what's going through my head right now.'

'Says who?'

The laughter died on her glossed lips, the same startling shade as her top, as she inched his coffee towards him with a decisive push of her finger.

'Drink up. The clock's ticking.'

Taking a gamble, he ignored the coffee, placed his index fingers against his temples and narrowed his eyes. 'Let me see…you're thinking how tired you are after working hard all day. You're thinking you can't wait to get out of here.'

She quirked an eyebrow and slow-clapped.

'Amazing. You should add a bit of crossing-over stuff to your repertoire, too.'

'I also see some cynical thoughts about me whizzing through your head. You don't want to hear what I have to say. You don't want to revisit the past. But maybe you're too scared to face how good we were together. And how we could have that again, given half a chance.'

Her finger convulsed on the edge of his saucer. 'Drink up. Then please leave.'

If she pushed the coffee any closer to him it would tip off the bar and splatter on his boots, and, reaching across he stilled her hand, vindicated by the slight tremor under his fingers, the flare of awareness in her eyes.

Cam might act as if she didn't give a flying fig about him anymore, but he knew better.

He'd seen it when she'd unconsciously leaned towards him a few minutes ago, he saw it now as her tongue darted out to moisten her full bottom lip, the ache to do the same almost visceral.

She'd always done that cute little tongue thing when nervous, like the first time he'd taken her kayaking down Rainbow Creek, the first time she'd tried trail-bike riding, arms clutched around his waist and hanging on for dear life, the first time she'd tried oysters au naturel at his coaxing, the first time they'd made love…

The memories flickered across his mind in crystal-clear clarity, sending a shard of pain stabbing at his gut, filling him with bittersweet regret.

He'd walked away from the best thing to happen to him, and, while he might not have had a choice back then, he sure had one now, and there was no way he'd let her go again.

'Not till we talk.'

Her chin tilted up in defiance as she snatched her hand out from under his and took a step back to distance herself from him. 'I suppose you're really not going to leave me alone till I agree?'

'That's right.'

'Still as stubborn as ever,' she muttered with a shake of her head.

'Good to see you remember so many things about me.'

His gaze dropped to the espresso in front of him, extra-strong black, just the way he liked it.

She shrugged, but not before he'd seen an answering gleam as if she remembered plenty.

'My mind has a habit of storing useless information. Don't take it personally.'

'I won't.'

He grinned, noticing an immediate softening around her mouth. She wanted to smile back, he could tell. They'd always been like this: he trying to charm her, she trying her utmost to pretend it wasn't working before giving in.

'How about we have this chat over a death by chocolate next door after you lock up?'

Her eyebrows shot up. 'You like the Chocolate Toad?'

'What's not to like? Great chocolate and a big, happy, green guy looking down on us while we talk.'

He leaned forward and crooked his finger at her, pleased when she met him halfway. 'You're not the only one who remembers things, you know. I bet chocolate is still your staple food.'

Camryn couldn't move.

She wanted to. Oh, yes, she wanted to run

away as fast as her boots would carry her, far from this man and the power he had over her.

After all she'd been through, after the pain of losing him, she should turn around right this very minute and walk away without a backward glance.

So why was she standing here, mesmerised by the twinkle in his eyes, captivated by his sense of humour, with the word 'yes' hovering on her lips?

'Come on. A girl deserves a good death by chocolate after a hard day's work. And I really think it's important you hear what I have to say.'

He leaned forward until their faces were inches apart, his clean, woodsy smell, as natural and outdoorsy as the rest of him, flooding her senses, tempting her to do crazy things as he had all those years ago. 'You know you want to.'

'Yes,' she breathed on a sigh, caught by his powers of persuasion and something more, something scary and indefinable. A soul-deep attraction to a man who set off sparks by simply tilting his head in acknowledgement had made her lose her mind and accept his invitation when nothing he could say would make up for what he'd done to her six years earlier.

'Great.'

He straightened, breaking the intimate spell woven around them. 'In that case I better bolt this coffee down, finish up my business and wait for you to close up.'

Business! She snapped her fingers, wondering how she could have forgotten her proposed meeting with the project manager.

'Actually, I've just remembered I'm meeting a project manager about some renovations I'm doing.'

'Best in the building industry, so I've been told.'

She raised an eyebrow. 'You obviously know Dirk and Mike, but I'm surprised the guys have been discussing my plans with you.'

His smile widened, his eyes twinkled, and her heart sank as realisation dawned.

'Why wouldn't they? I'm the best project manager around. Ask anybody.'

His reappearance must have really thrown her if she'd missed the connection between him turning up here, knowing the guys and her scheduled meeting. Talk about slow on the uptake, but, somehow, she didn't care a toss about anything but how let down she felt.

He'd said he'd come here to see her but it was obviously for business reasons. And of course he'd have to mention their shared past, smooth the way if she were to hire him. She'd been such a fool. Again.

'I know what you're thinking, but don't. Just for the record, I came here to see you, to talk to you. As for you needing a project manager, that was my trump card if you'd tried to boot me out the door the minute I set foot in here.'

There he went again, reading her so easily, and she quickly slid an impassive mask into place, knowing it was too late.

Okay, so he wasn't just here on business, but that didn't change facts: she'd loved him, he'd walked out on her, and there wasn't one damn thing he could say to change that.

'Come on, Cam. Catching up can't hurt. And if I can help out with your renovations, all the better.'

She still had time to fob him off, to come to her senses, to give him some feeble excuse why she'd rather pick up a sledge hammer and bang the walls down herself than have him involved in her renovations.

But that was the coward's way out, and if she'd learned anything since she'd arrived in Melbourne as a naïve nineteen-year-old ready to take on the world while mending a broken heart, it was to face things head on.

Besides, she needed the renovations completed sooner rather than later or she'd lose out on the chance at expansion into the apartment next to hers. She'd lived in what she affectionately termed her 'shoebox' since she'd opened the café, pouring all her funds into making the Niche great. But with the café doing better and the opportunity to enlarge her living space, she had to strike now. However, she'd been given the run around and time was running out.

She needed his skills asap, and, now he was here, she should at least hear what he had to say—regarding business only, that was.

With a resigned sigh, she glanced at her watch. 'I'll meet you next door in forty-five minutes,' she said, half hoping he'd renege once he heard how long he'd have to wait. The other half of her was already doing a mental scrummage through her handbag for lipgloss, pressed powder compact, brush and hair serum, essentials she'd need to make herself halfway presentable for their date.

Date?

Business or otherwise, she'd agreed to go on a date.

With Blane Andrews, the guy who'd left her with a broken heart without a backward glance.

Was she *nuts*?

'Forty-five minutes it is.'

He lifted his coffee cup towards her in a toasting action before strolling away, his even-paced strides achingly familiar. Blane in all his laid-back glory never hurried anywhere.

Unless she counted how fast he'd run out on her.

Wincing at the memory, she got busy with the day's takings, did a final check for tomorrow's bookings, determinedly avoiding looking at the table where the occasional low rumble of laughter emanated from.

She focused on the booking diary and accompanying table sketches, running her finger down the list of names, matching them to the table numbers, but the figures blurred and danced the harder she stared at them, and, finally relenting, she allowed her gaze to drift upwards.

Either Blane had been staring at her all along or he was doing his mind-reading trick again, for the second she looked up their gazes locked and held, an unexpected rush of heat flooding her body, making her tummy quiver and her legs tremble so hard she had to grip onto the bar for support.

He smiled, a slow, sensual upward curving of his lips, a smile designed solely for her, a smile that was temptation personified.

She didn't stand a chance.

No matter how often she told herself this was just a quick catch-up supper while they discussed business, no matter how hard she tried to believe she wasn't doing this because she was curious to hear his excuse for what he'd done, no matter how much she wanted to turn him away, to hurt him as he'd hurt her six years ago, she knew, beyond a shadow of a doubt, that Blane

Andrews, in all his tempting glory, still intrigued her enough to sit down over her favourite dessert after all this time…with her husband.

CHAPTER TWO

'WHAT? You've seen me eat chocolate before.'

'Not with such gusto. It's cute.'

Camryn waved her fork in the air, enjoying this way too much. Not just the death by chocolate sampler platter, which was to die for, but the easy-going camaraderie that had sprung up between her and Blane with little effort.

She'd been determined to discuss business, scoff down her chocolate and bolt out the door. Instead, they'd made desultory small talk over hot mochas, loosened up through sensational almond biscotti and were presently at the comfortable 'let's sit back, relax and avoid any potential minefields' stage.

'So what you're really saying is I'm a pig.'

He shook his head and dug his fork into a

massive wedge of mud cake. 'You're trying to get me into trouble.'

'Am I?'

She sent him her best innocent smile and forked another mouth-watering, melt-on-her-tongue, divine piece of choc-orange mousse cake into her mouth.

'Oh, yeah.'

He couldn't take his eyes off her, and, rather than being disconcerted, she was enjoying the attention way too much.

'From where I'm sitting, it looks like you're already in trouble.'

Big trouble, the kind of trouble that couldn't be explained away no matter how hard he tried or what he said.

Yet the longer she sat here, more relaxed than she'd been in ages, she couldn't summon up the animosity his actions of six years ago deserved.

Shoving more cake into her mouth, she flicked her tongue out to catch a crumb clinging to her top lip, the spark of excitement in his eyes as they riveted to her mouth sending heat streaking through her body in a way she hadn't experienced since…for ever.

After a long, loaded moment he blinked, his eyes crinkling with the smile never far from his face.

'Look, I know you want to talk about your renovations and that's probably the only reason you agreed to meet me here, and I promise you we will talk business later, but now I've buttered you up with your favourite food, I want to tell you what this is all about.'

Just like that, the smooth chocolate mousse solidified into an indigestible lump in her stomach.

What was she doing, play-acting as if everything was fine and she was on some kind of date?

Blane was her husband.

Who she hadn't seen in six long years.

She should be grilling him, not noticing the sexy new grooves bracketing his mouth, the laugh-lines that had multiplied around those striking eyes, and his penchant for rubbing the back of his neck when she put him on the spot.

'If you've softened me up with chocolate, what you have to say must be pretty bad.'

It had better be, for she'd accept nothing less than a catastrophe on the scale of Melbourne City

Council shutting down every café in the Docklands as an excuse for what he'd done to her.

He held his hand out, and it wavered in a so-so gesture. 'Considering I've spent the last six years thinking about you, wondering if I did the right thing, wishing there'd been some other way, I don't think it's all bad.'

'Let me be the judge of that.'

She sat back and folded her arms, resisting the urge to hug them around her middle for what scant comfort she could get.

His smile faded, and, crazily, irrationally, she missed it. He'd rarely been serious when they'd first met, making her laugh every chance he'd got, and it looked as if nothing had changed. Ever since he'd waltzed into the café a few hours ago he'd been smiling, which explained why she could barely think straight.

His smile had been her undoing in the past—that and his boyish charm, his sensitivity, his warmth, his passion…

Gulping a healthy lungful of air to ease the pain in her chest, she tried to focus before she did something crazy—like tell him it didn't matter where he'd been or why as long as he'd come back.

'Go ahead, tell me. Give it to me straight, I'm a big girl, I can take it.'

Regret clouded his eyes as he reached across and held out his hand, silently imploring her to take it. But she couldn't. Not if she wanted to remain detached long enough to hear him out and put an end to this unwise evening.

'I need you to understand why I left.'

'So you can ease your conscience?'

He withdrew his hand, folding his arms in a posture mirroring hers, sadness ageing him beyond his twenty-seven years.

'This isn't about making me feel better.'

'Then what's it about?'

He pinned her with a direct stare, his eyes steely pewter in the soft candlelight from a corny red-heart tea-light burning low in the centre of the table.

'Us.'

Camryn swallowed the lump of emotion lodged in her throat. How could one tiny word hold so much pain, so many memories?

Us.

Cam and Blane against the world.

Young, impetuous, with the world at their feet, dreams to follow, places to be. Fun to be had, life to be lived to the fullest, the two of them egging each other on, the exhilarating surge of love a maelstrom that propelled them straight into marriage before they could catch their breath.

Whether sharing a quiet cappuccino at the end of a working day, streaking towards the creek to see who'd jump in first, or hiking to the top of nearby Rainbow Mountain for some private canoodling time or dashing after the first daisy he'd plucked for her as it swirled away on a warm summer's breeze, it had been the two of them, laughing so hard they could barely catch their breath, loving so fiercely and vividly and profoundly.

It had been like that right from the very beginning, the impetuous, precipitous, thrilling rush of loving this man.

The breathtaking high of being a couple ready to take on the world together, to the lowest of lows as she'd plummeted into the depths of despair when he'd left.

Blinking to stave off the sting of tears, she focused on a single crumb lying rather pathetically in her lap, all on its own. Just like her.

Great. Now she was comparing herself to cake crumbs.

This wasn't a good idea. She needed to get out of here before she broke down in front of him, showing him exactly how much he still affected her.

He must have anticipated her urge to bolt because he rushed on. 'Those three months in Rainbow Creek were the best of my life. You were the best thing to ever happen to me.'

Her gaze snapped up to his, harsh and accusatory. 'Then why did you leave?'

He had the grace to look aggrieved. 'Because we were too young. Because we would've changed and grown apart. Because I wondered if you really loved me or were using me as an escape route out of town and a way to rebel against your parents. But mostly because you would've put your dreams on hold for mine and I couldn't live with that. You deserved better.'

'*What?*'

She shook her head, trying to clear it.

She could have sworn he'd just said he'd left because of her, as if he'd been doing her some great favour. Of all the lousy, stupid excuses…

'You left because of *me*?'

Her blood boiled, and she slammed her hands palm down on the table. Bad move. It gave him the opportunity to reach out and cover one of her hands with his, his soothing touch too warm, too comfortable.

But she didn't shrug him off. She couldn't, because somehow with that one touch he'd broken something inside her, some inner reserve of animosity she'd been harbouring against him ever since he'd walked out of Rainbow Creek.

And she didn't want to resent him or be bitter or harbour any grudges. She wanted a real, honest-to-goodness explanation, a reason that would finally set her free so she could move on.

'Cam, look at me.'

He squeezed her hand gently and she gnawed on her bottom lip, blinking furiously.

She wouldn't cry in front of him. She couldn't,

for she had a feeling once the flood gates opened she'd cry enough tears to fill Port Phillip Bay.

Taking a deep breath, she raised her eyes to meet his, her heart clenching at the sincerity blazing in his.

'I was selfish in marrying you. I wanted you so badly I was blinded to anything else. You were only nineteen, for goodness' sake, and had spent your whole life in that small town. I took advantage of you.'

He rubbed his free hand over his face but it did little to wipe the anguish off his face. 'We were practically kids. And eloping? Blowing off your parents? Going against their wishes? What were we thinking?'

'I married you because I wanted to,' she said, her voice tremulous, and she swallowed several times to stop it cracking completely. 'You were my world.'

Pain, deep and irreversible, flickered in his eyes, turning them stormy pewter as he gripped onto her hand as if he'd never let go.

'Same here, sweetheart, same here. But you wanted to follow me, hit the road to goodness knows where while I scrounged for work, when you had your own dreams to follow.'

He jerked his thumb over his shoulder towards the café next door. 'There's your dream right there. You wanted to live in the big city and run your own place; you've done it. And that's great. You couldn't have done that if you'd traipsed around with me to the ends of the earth and back. I couldn't let you do it.'

Something niggled in the back of her mind, something about her parents, but she ignored it for now, needing to concentrate long enough to make sense of what he'd just said, to absorb the emotional impact of it all.

For there wasn't a doubt in her mind that Blane meant every word he said, that he truly believed he'd done the right thing.

But at what cost? Her heart? The wonderful life they could have had together?

'You couldn't *let* me?'

She shook her head, hoping she could get through this without dissolving into a teary mess.

'It was *my* choice to make. Mine, not yours. At the very least we should've discussed it…' She trailed off as a light bulb flashed in her mind, illuminating what she'd been trying to put her finger on a few moments ago. 'How did you know I was going against my parents' wishes? They never spoke to you about what they wanted. You didn't even see them the week after we eloped.'

Guilt clouded the strong, rugged features she'd once loved with all her heart, and her hand shook with the effort not to reach out and smooth the indentation from between his brows.

'I went to see them after we eloped to try and explain how we really felt about each other, how I'd never try and come between you and them.'

'Bet that went down a treat,' she muttered, struck by the irony of the situation. In leaving town, he'd catapulted her into a life-changing confrontation with her parents, resulting in an estrangement she couldn't breach.

'They gave it to me straight, and I knew then I couldn't put my needs ahead of yours. It wasn't right or fair. And they were right about one thing: I had nothing to offer you. You had a comfortable life there, a way of building a financial future before following your own dreams, and I couldn't take that away from you.'

A harsh snort burst from deep within, and she took advantage of his momentary surprise to ease her hand out from under his. She had to before she turned hers palm up and hung on for dear life.

'Funnily enough, you leaving ended up being the catalyst in me running from Rainbow Creek as fast I could.'

Shock widened his pupils. 'Why?'

Camryn took a sip of water, instantly transported back to that day in her parents' kitchen: the tantrum, the accusations, and the god-awful truth.

'I lost it. Blew up at them big time. Mum lost it, too, we started arguing, then she hurls in my face this was the very reason she was keeping Nan's inheritance from me till I turned twenty-one.'

She slugged the rest of the water, hoping to wash away the bitter taste of her parents' deception, lingering to this day.

'Turns out I could've had the money when I reached eighteen. Imagine how different our— my life could've been.'

And that was what rankled the most. If she'd

had the money when she'd been entitled, maybe they would still be together. He wouldn't have had to scrape by from job to job, town to town; they could have had a healthy start to their marriage with enough capital to do whatever they wanted.

But her parents had robbed her of that opportunity, had stolen the kind of life she and Blane had talked about while lying under the stars beside the river in Rainbow Creek, two young lovers daring to dream.

And she'd never forgive them for that.

'I'm sorry.'

He reached out and touched her cheek, a soft, comforting gesture, all too fleeting when he withdrew his hand. 'For everything.'

Tears scalded the back of her eyes, hot, burning tears that threatened to spill out and run down her cheeks in a cascading waterfall.

Shaking her head, she used her hair as a shield, grateful she'd had the common sense to release it from its plait.

It didn't work, as he reached forward and gently tucked a few curly strands behind her left ear.

'I know this has been tough, listening to all this heavy stuff. But we had to have this conversation, Cam. It's the only way we can move forward.'

Her gaze snapped to his, her belly tumbling into a sickening free-for-all as she registered what he meant.

Moving forward.

He'd met someone.

Someone important enough for him to hunt her down, soften her up with his sob story, then demand a divorce?

As if sensing her distress, he cupped her chin and leaned forward, his face scant inches from hers.

'I really want to move forward. With you.'

Her angst dissipated in an instant, dissolving on a wave of such intense longing she could have quite happily flung herself into his arms across the table and never let go.

Before her common sense kicked in. What was she thinking, considering taking another chance on a guy like Blane?

Sure, his reasons for leaving sounded sincere, and a small part of her agreed they'd probably been too young, too crazy in eloping, but going down that road again after all this time? He'd also been right about the fact they'd both changed and they had grown apart—thanks to him.

'I can't.'

Hurt flickered in his eyes, the smoky-blue flecks shimmering, and she reached out to touch his cheek before she could stop herself.

She'd meant her touch to be innocuous, a brief touch on his cheek to prove a point. However, she hadn't banked on the urge to linger, the tiny prickles of whisker beckoning her to explore, to trace the contours of his cheek with her finger-tips ever-so-slowly just as she used to.

Nor had she counted on him capturing her hand, gently scraping her fingers across his cheek, as if trying to imprint the feel of him into her palm.

'You sure about that?'

She jerked back, withdrawing her hand with the finesse of a wounded rhino, ignoring the questioning gleam in his steady gaze.

'Because, the way I see it, we're still married. We still have chemistry, and you still care as much as I do, otherwise why agree to meet me here?'

She'd been asking herself the very same question since she'd agreed to this foolhardy evening.

'Because you wanted a chance to explain, and I'm a decent enough person to give it to you. But that's as far as it goes.'

He shook his head, the corners of his mouth curling into that devastating smile he used to his advantage. What hope did a girl have?

'Sorry. I'm not buying it.'

'Fine. You want to know the truth? I said yes because I've wasted enough time looking for you, and now that you're here it's a good opportunity to get divorced and move on.'

He should have bristled, or been angry, or defensive, or…something!

Instead, he sat back, looking way too relaxed for a guy who was just about to go through what for most people was a major life-changing event. Apparently divorce ranked right up there with death of a spouse and moving house; considering she'd already been through both those cataclysmic events six years ago—losing Blane had been akin to him dying in the devastation stakes—she knew firsthand how rough it could be.

'You looked for me?'

No acknowledgement of what she'd said about the divorce, just a hint of curiosity as he leaned forward and placed his arms on the table.

He had strong forearms, lean yet muscular, with a light sprinkling of dark hair, forearms she'd trailed her fingers over when she'd explored his body for the first time, forearms that had lifted her up and swung her around after they'd married, forearms that had cradled her close on their honeymoon night spent in a dingy motel on the outskirts of Echuca.

It had been all they could afford, but it hadn't mattered. Not the annoying neon sign that flashed on some crazy cycle, not the sagging mattress, not the grungy brown carpet in their room. All of it had faded into oblivion when they'd fallen into each other's arms for the first time as man and wife.

It was a lifetime ago, in her past, so why was she suddenly all too aware of the underlying buzz of electricity still flowing between them?

'Yeah, I looked for you, for about a year. You know, to serve you *divorce* papers.'

'Only a year, huh?'

Once again he ignored the D word hanging between them, and strangely enough it didn't seem all that important anymore with his steady grey-eyed gaze fixed on her, her skin tingling as if he'd physically touched her.

She made a frantic grab at her plait before belatedly remembering she'd let her hair down—metaphorically only, she hoped!

'I like your hair better this way.'

Before she could blink, he'd reached out and captured a strand of her hair, gently twirling it around his index finger, forming a loose curl before releasing it, his fingertips brushing her shoulder as he sat back, a wistful expression on his face.

Clamping down the urge to yank his hands across the table and shove them through her hair, she shrugged, trying to ignore her burning, yearning skin where he'd briefly touched her.

'Having long hair in the hospitality industry is impractical. I have to wear it tied back all the time.'

'As long as you get to let it down once in a while.'

Was he asking if she had a social life, if she'd dated?

Hmm…if she counted the catch-up coffee with Lars the Lech and the dinner from hell with Deon the Drag, yeah, she'd dated. Twice in six years, two times too many, for neither of those guys had been Blane, neither had come close to sparking her interest as the man sitting across from her did.

'I'm a self-confessed workaholic. I want the café to be the best, and to do that I need to put in the hard yards.'

'Work isn't everything.'

Camryn couldn't explain the sudden change in atmosphere. One minute he was laid-back and laughing at her, the next he'd tensed up, from his bunched shoulders to his folded arms.

She topped up her water glass from the funky red glass bottle in the middle of the table, making a mental note to look for something similar for the Niche.

'It is for me.'

He paused, as if weighing his words carefully, and it was the first time she'd seen him look anything but relaxed all evening.

'I guess I'm trying to find out if there's anyone else in the picture.'

The smart thing to do would be to fob him off, maybe even tell a little white lie to cement their estrangement and obtain the divorce she should have got years ago.

Instead, she stalled for time, forking the last piece of cake into her mouth and sighing as the chocolate mousse melted on her tongue, releasing a citrus burst in tart contrast to the luscious sweetness.

'Come on, Cam, it's a simple question.'

'There's no one else.'

She cleared her throat, blaming her husky tone on a stray cake crumb rather than the sick thought that he'd probably dated—and extensively. 'What about you?'

Not that it was any of her business. Not that it mattered. She was just curious…

He unfolded his arms to lean forward and place them on the table, way too close to hers, lowering his tone to match hers.

'There's been no one else for me, only you. It's always been you,' he murmured, sliding his hand to cover hers, his calloused palm rasping across her delicate skin and sending shivers shooting up her arm.

His heartrending statement hung in the air as waiters bustled around them, cake plates were whisked from kitchen to table, and the steady buzz of patrons filled the air along with the sound of muted jazz.

He leaned closer, his forearm brushing hers again, and she clenched her teeth to refrain from sighing with longing.

'Look, you know I'm a stand-up guy, and I'm too old to play games, so I'll give it to you straight. I want us to get to know each other again. Take our time. It can be dinner, a movie, another coffee, whatever. The ball's in your court.'

She sat there, transfixed by the sincerity in his tone, by his guileless grey eyes, by the tiny spark of electricity arcing from his forearm to hers.

Was he for real?

Did he want to give them a second chance?

Or was this just one of those times where he was passing through Melbourne, found himself single, and thought he'd look up a former flame for old time's sake?

She might be the ultimate city girl these days with the street savvy to match, but it was times like this she wondered if shy Cammie from Rainbow Creek came out to play, filling her with insecurities and doubts and self-recrimination.

A huge part of her wanted to shout yes to getting reacquainted, though she wasn't that naïve. She may be singing the divorce tune, but spending even the shortest amount of time in Blane's company in years had her hormones sitting up, taking notice, and screaming 'take me, I'm still all yours'.

She'd never experienced with anyone else the kind of 'in your face' physical attraction they had, the kind that made her body go into meltdown with the slightest touch, the kind that could make a girl lose sight of how far she'd come, and lose sight of her goals.

And if there was one thing she'd learned after leaving her old life behind, it was to stay focused on her goals.

With that in mind she sat back, reclaiming her personal space and what was left of her common sense. 'I didn't want this meeting to be about us. I wanted to talk business.'

Disappointment clouded his eyes momentarily

as he registered she hadn't given him a direct response. To his credit, he took it like the man she knew him to be and slid his resident smile back into place, the one which crinkled his eyes adorably.

'The way I see it, there's not much to talk about. The guys filled me in on what you need, I'm your man. It's that simple.'

Simple? Was the guy nuts?

There was nothing remotely simple about this, any of it. Having him turn up out of the blue, asking for a second chance, her desperation to get her renovations done…no, simple didn't begin to describe the position she now found herself in.

'But what if…' She bit down on her bottom lip, unsure whether to be blunt and drive him away completely or ignore the giveaway pitter-patter of her heart whenever he smiled and remain focused on the business aspect of their dealings.

'What if you don't want to have anything to do with me personally but want to take advantage of me professionally?'

She blushed, not surprised he knew her so well. He'd always done that, finished her sentences, read her thoughts. After such a short time together, it shouldn't have been that easy.

But it had been, which made it all the harder to ignore the tiny flicker of hope his proposal had elicited earlier.

Could they give their marriage a second chance?

At that moment a child at a nearby table let out a delighted squeal as a waiter placed a 'frog in the pond' in front of her, her blue eyes wide with wonder as she peered at the chocolate frog suspended in green jelly, and Camryn's blood instantly chilled.

She watched, transfixed, as the little girl's mother leaned over and gave her a sloppy smooch on her forehead while her father ruffled her mop of blonde curls, their love obvious—the complete, perfect family.

Something she could never have.

Something she'd had no idea how badly she'd wanted till the option had been taken away from her, cruelly wrenched bit by bit with every visit to the hospital in the years since she'd lost Blane, a stark reminder that everything that truly mattered to her was gone.

Her husband.

Her parents.

Her fertility.

While she'd learned to focus on her goals and block out the pain of loss, seeing Blane now, hearing him confirm she still meant something to him, only served to reinforce what she'd known since the last surgery: she couldn't have kids, and it wouldn't be fair on any man, particularly one she'd once loved as much as she'd loved him, to have to deal with that.

'Hey, you okay? Sorry if I've come on a bit strong.'

He reached out and laid a hand on her shoulder, wrenching her attention back to him and away from the happy family scene tugging at her heartstrings.

Momentarily comforted by his touch before coming to her senses and realising she had no right to be, she gently shrugged off his hand on the pretext of reaching for her bag.

'Look, can you give me some time to think about all this? I'll get back to you about the project manager position.'

As if.

The moment she left this place she had no intention of ever getting in touch with him ever again.

Her nerves were flayed, her memories too poignant, her pain raw, and she couldn't see any point in prolonging the inevitable: them parting ways for good.

He rummaged in his back pocket, pulled out his wallet, and handed her a business card, bearing his name, mobile number and email on rather plain but expensive cream cardboard.

'Here's where you can reach me. *When* you call.'

She managed a small smile at his confidence, took the card and slid it into the back pocket of her jeans, knowing she wouldn't use it, wishing she could.

It was prevaricating like this that could get her into serious trouble, and she needed to get out of here before those sexy grey eyes with their blue flecks and endearing corner crinkles, along with accompanying ingenuous smile, undermined her completely.

'I have to get going. It's been a big day and I need to crash before starting all over again tomorrow.'

'Sure.'

He slid several notes onto the table before she could reach for her purse, and he held up a hand when she opened her mouth to protest.

'My shout. I asked you to come, I want to pay. Besides, you never know when I might need a snappy espresso fix again, and I want to keep the proprietor of that great place next door happy.'

'Flattery will get you everywhere,' she said, secretly thrilled by his chivalry in insisting on paying, remembering the old times they'd had to go Dutch because neither of them had a spare cent to their names.

'Will it?'

'What can I say? The café's my baby.'

'You have every right to be proud. It's a great place.'

He took hold of her hand as if it were the most natural thing in the world, his touch warm and steady, infusing her with a sense of security she hadn't known in a long time.

'I know.'

This wasn't a time for false modesty. She knew the Niche was fabulous, from its cosy corner, bearing low leather sofas in the softest fawn surrounded by comfortable matching ottomans and strategically placed fuchsia and turquoise bolster cushions, to the monstrous timber bar topped by stainless steel with its co-ordinated bar stools.

She loved every inch of the place, with its exquisite water views on one side, to the views of Melbourne's city skyline on the other. She'd built it up from scratch, competing in a high-end hospitality market, and could now proudly say it held its own.

Quite simply, the Niche was exactly that for her: a niche in Melbourne, a personal space, a home. Something she'd craved since leaving Rainbow Creek, something concrete and solid and all hers to fill the aching void deep in her heart.

He squeezed her hand, understanding exactly where she was coming from. He should; she'd bared her soul to him, poured out her hopes and dreams about owning a place just like the Niche all those years ago.

Pity he hadn't listened to her other dream that had involved 'till death us do part'.

'Would you like me to take you home?'

'No, but thanks for offering. Still the gentleman, huh?'

In a rash, spur of the moment gesture she didn't rationalise and would probably regret later, she leaned forward and placed a quick peck on his cheek, fighting the urge to linger.

His stubble prickled her lips, leaving them tingling and hypersensitive as she inhaled deeply, savouring his scent. Crushed leaves, cedar, the woodsy cedar instantly transporting her back to Rainbow Creek and the huge cedar tree with its old rubber tyre she used to swing on in her parents' backyard where he'd pushed her for hours one sultry Sunday afternoon.

It was a safe smell, an evocative smell, and she pulled away sharply before she did something even crazier like fling herself into his arms, just like she used to run from the swing into his open, waiting arms.

'I guess there's something to be said for old-fashioned manners if that's the type of response I get,' he said, rubbing his cheek where she'd left the faintest lipstick mark, a goofy grin on his face.

Her heart hitched at the familiarity of his ex-

pression, the same loopy way he'd looked at her
when she'd served him the very first day they'd
met, and she swayed towards him, torn between
wanting to fling herself into his arms and resur-
rect the good old days and run as far from him
as she could get.

Pulling up short, she stiffened, hoping he
hadn't read the yearning in her face. 'I don't
have far to go.'

'Okay, then. I guess we'll call it a night.'

'Uh-huh.'

'Thanks for agreeing to meet with me, Cam.'

She held her breath as he leaned towards her,
his head descending slowly, her heart pounding
in anticipation of a goodnight kiss she shouldn't
want so damn much.

He took his time, and she clenched her hands
into fists to stop from reaching out, bunching his
T-shirt and yanking him towards her.

Her eyelids fluttered shut, and she tilted her
face up, silently praying he'd go for her lips,
guessing he'd play the gentleman to the end and
settle for her cheek after all this time.

'You have my card. Use it,' he whispered

against her ear, his warm breath tickling the sensitive skin behind her lobe and sending tiny shivers of desire down her spine.

Her eyes flew open to find him staring at her with way too much perception, as if he knew what she wanted but would make her wait for it.

Well, he'd be waiting a long time considering she had no intention of using his card.

'See you.'

Her noncommittal reply fell on deaf ears as his confident smile broadened, and she sent him a jaunty wave as she strolled away, resisting the urge to peek over her shoulder to see if he was watching her. By the heat burning holes in her back and spreading, he was, but she didn't look back.

Just like he hadn't when he'd left her high and dry and walked out on her in Rainbow Creek.

CHAPTER THREE

CAMRYN gnawed on her bottom lip, giving the screwdriver an extra vicious twist as she tried to fix the refrigerator door for the third time.

The screwdriver slipped, sheering off the hinge and gouging a deep gash into the pale oak cabinet housing the fridge, and she swore, shoving the useless tool back into the pink tool case designed especially for 'the independent woman'.

'Is it the *bloody tool* that's the problem or the supposed expert wielding it?'

She narrowed her eyes, sending Anna a glare she reserved for rude customers. 'I never said I was an expert.'

'No? Then what's with the fancy tools?'

Anna's grin widened as Camryn sprang up from her squatting position and kicked the offending tool case under the bench.

'Apparently they're only good for hammering the odd picture hook or tightening the odd loose screw.' Which was exactly what she had—quite a few loose screws if she thought she could fix something requiring bigger biceps than hers.

'As for fixing fridge hinges…' She blew out an exasperated puff of air, casting a malevolent glance at the offending metal hinge. 'I hate having to call a handyman just to fix something as small as this.'

'But if you don't, we'll lose tomorrow's cheesecake supply.' Anna paused, tapping an apricot-coloured fingernail against her bottom lip. 'Know anyone we can call at short notice?'

Camryn's heart sank.

She knew someone all right.

In fact, his business card had been burning a hole in her pocket all week.

She'd had no intention of calling Blane, despite the fact she did a double-take every time a tradesman entered the café and she'd dreamed of his laid-back charming smile and twinkling grey eyes several nights since.

In fact, she should have thrown his card out and

would have if she'd been able to find it, but she had so many pairs of jeans she rotated as her 'uniform' that she'd forgotten which pair she'd worn the night he'd waltzed back into her life.

She'd assumed she'd washed them anyway and that would have taken care of that, but, as fate would have it, when she'd crouched down to fix the hinge, something had crackled in her back pocket, and she'd found his card.

If she believed in all that airy-fairy fate rubbish she would say she was meant to call him. But she didn't, so she'd put it down to luck instead.

She needed a handyman, she'd found his card, she'd call him. That was where it would end.

And if he tried charming her again, she'd plead work and hide out in the back storeroom till he finished the job.

'So, do you know anyone? Huh? Huh?'

Anna had been trying to get the low-down on her supper with Blane all week, and Camryn had told her the basics: they'd eaten, they'd chatted, they'd parted company, end of story. Looked like she was about to open a new chapter. Of course, she'd omitted the teensy-weensy detail of him being her husband. What was the point of going into all that when he wouldn't be for much longer?

'Hold on to your latte, funny girl. I'll give Blane a call now and see if he can swing by tonight.'

Anna's wide grin spoke volumes: she wasn't buying her casual attitude one bit.

'Good idea. I'm sure Blane will be a lot more skilled with his tools.'

Rolling her eyes, she couldn't help but chuckle at the innuendo. 'We can only hope.'

Turning away, she slid her fingers into her back pocket, relieved and scared at the same time when they wrapped around the stiff cardboard.

She didn't want to do this, she really didn't, but the café came first, and if she wanted to offer her regular patrons their fix of the best cheesecake this side of the Docklands, she had no choice.

Pulling the card quickly out of her pocket, she stared at the crisp, bold font, BLANE ANDREWS, amongst the crinkles.

How many times had she absentmindedly doodled Camryn Andrews over the years? Not many, considering he'd ditched her so fast after they'd married she hadn't had time to get around to officially changing her name.

'Just ring him already!'

Sighing, she reached for the phone, her thumb poised over the touch buttons while she flipped the card over and over with her other hand.

'Why don't you go check on the latest Java bean shipment then head on home? I'll be fine.'

'I'm sure you will.'

Anna smirked, sending a pointed look at the card in her hand. 'I'm sure Blane is very handy with a tool or two.'

She rolled her eyes. 'Enough with the tool jokes, already. Now, go.'

She wanted to be alone when she made the call, not trusting herself to feign nonchalance under Anna's astute gaze when she heard his voice again.

'Okay, boss. Catch you tomorrow.'

She waited till Anna had headed through to the storeroom before glancing at the card and punching in the number for Blane's mobile, hoping he'd answer for the sake of her cheesecakes, hoping he wouldn't for her peace of mind.

Her heart stalled as the dial tone was replaced by the crackle of static before 'Blane Andrews speaking' filtered down the line in that deep, mellifluous tone she knew all too well.

'Hi, it's me. How are you?'

She stiffened at the slight pause before willing herself to relax, thankful it gave her a moment to take a deep breath and slow down her thudding heart.

'Hey, Cam. I'm fine. And glad you called.'

Cringing as she steadied herself to burst his bubble of hope, as she'd called for another reason than what he wished for, she rushed on. 'Actually, I need your help. I've got a refrigerator hinge that needs fixing, and it's pretty urgent. I gave it a shot myself but couldn't manage it, so I was wondering if you could pop around tonight and take a look for me?'

The sound of a circular saw whined in the background, closely followed by a loud hammering that had her holding the phone an inch away from her ear.

'Sure. Let me finish up here and I'll be around in about two hours.'

To give him credit, he didn't sound disappointed or annoyed. She should have been relieved. Instead, a small part of her was insulted he didn't push her for an explanation as to why she hadn't called or when she finally did it was to ask him for his building expertise.

Injecting false cheer into her voice, she said, 'Great. I really appreciate it.'

'No worries, see you later.'

He hung up first, leaving her staring at the phone in confusion.

By his own admission he wanted them to get reacquainted. He'd said it, blunt as you like, the other night. So why wasn't he bothered she hadn't called?

Shaking her head, she replaced the cordless phone in its charger and crumpled the card in her hand. Considering almost a week had lapsed since their infamous chat, he'd clearly got the message she wasn't interested in resurrecting the past.

Great.

Or was it?

Blane slid his mobile back into his top pocket, rubbed his palms down the side of his jeans, and perched on the tailgate of his ute.

'Well, I'll be damned,' he muttered, his words whipped away by the blustery gale blowing straight off the ocean, the wind effectively drowning out Mike's staple gun as it hammered nails into the fence.

She'd called.

After six days, during which time he'd mentally kicked himself for being a jackass and leaving the ball in her court, she'd finally picked up the phone.

Okay, so it wasn't quite the 'let's catch up and have a drink, dinner, whatever' call he'd been hoping for, but she'd called nonetheless.

A busted fridge hinge could be fixed by anybody, but she'd rung him, which could mean one of two things: she wanted to see him again and was using the fix-it as a flimsy excuse, or she couldn't be bothered paying some guy out of the phone book a small fortune for such a quick job and was using their shared past to get what she wanted: a fixed fridge.

Shaking his head, he inhaled deeply, hoping a good lungful of bracing sea air might give him the clarity he'd so desperately sought since he'd first laid eyes on Cam again.

Refreshing as it was, the tang of salty sea air didn't help as memories of the way she'd looked and smiled and sounded assailed him.

Memories of those incredibly tight black jeans moulding her long legs to perfection, those sexy knee-high boots, her hair loose and flowing around her shoulders when she'd let it out, the same rich colour as the chocolate fountain on the bar of her café.

She'd changed so much, the young, shy girl maturing into a confident, stunning woman. If she'd captivated him six years ago, it had nothing on the need coursing through him now, the need to reconcile with his wife.

His *wife*…the word rolled around and around in his brain, sweet and tempting and oh-so-right, exactly like Cam herself.

She'd been his driving force all these years, the thought of coming back to her with so much more to offer making him work longer, harder and faster than his competitors.

Reuniting with the only woman in the world for him had been a powerful motivator, and now that he'd finally seen her…well, he wouldn't take no for an answer.

Cam could stall and bluster and pretend she was immune to him all she liked, but he knew better.

He'd seen the old spark in her eyes, the tenderness when she'd swayed towards him, the flare of desire when he'd touched her.

He hadn't sugar-coated why he'd left, and while she probably hadn't accepted it yet, she'd come around.

In the meantime he had every intention of giving her all the encouragement in the world to see exactly how perfect they could be together. All over again.

And if she needed concrete proof… Glancing at the house, he hopped off the ute, refastened his tool belt and sauntered back to work, whistling 'Fly Me to the Moon', their song, under his breath with a smile on his face and hope in his heart.

Camryn paced the length of the bar, her highheeled boots rapping against the polished boards, echoing in the silence.

She'd flicked on the music, her favourite swing singer, only to switch it off again in a mild panic when *their* song had come on, as Blane might see it as a sign she wanted to create a cosy atmosphere or, worse, take it as an indication she'd changed her mind.

She'd retied her hair into its signature French braid, blown out all the tea-light candles, switched on the bright fluorescent strip hanging over the bar, and removed all traces of the essential oil she'd been burning since closing, all in an attempt to 'de-cosy' the place.

The last thing she needed was him getting the wrong idea.

Which was?

An image instantly sprang to mind of the two of them sitting in the plush lounge area of the café situated towards the back, curled up on one of the comfy sofas, sharing a steaming moccaccino, or maybe one of the fine Merlots she kept out the back, with the lamps muted and the luscious aromas of cinnamon and vanilla in the air from the essential oils she used to complement the baking.

Oh, yeah, she could see it all too clearly, and unfortunately her vision of the wrong idea appeared way too right.

Casting one last critical look around—and satisfied she'd obliterated any semblance of romantic ambience—she fiddled with the espresso machine, going through the soothing motions of pouring milk into a stainless-steel jug, sliding it under the frother, filling the scoop with coffee, using the tamper, checking the water level.

The familiar actions calmed her, giving her something to do with her hands rather than tug on her plait till it unravelled.

She had nothing to be nervous about. Absolutely nothing. This was business. Nothing to do with pleasure at all.

With a groan, her head fell forward and thunked against the espresso machine. It was the thought combination of Blane and pleasure that did it.

Of course, he had to find her like this, with her head slumped against the machine, his rapid knock snapping her head to attention in time to see his face creased with concern as he peered through the glass door with hands cupped against it.

Giving her head a rueful rub, she crossed to the door and unlocked it, beckoning him in.

'You okay?'

She ushered him in before relocking the door. 'Yeah, fine. I was just inventing a new way to check the coffee-ground levels.'

He smiled, his dubious expression saying he didn't believe her for a second. But what could she tell him? The mere thought of seeing him had her in a spin, wishing she could clunk her head against a hard surface repeatedly to knock some sense into herself?

'How have you been?'

He propped against the bar, giving her a tempting view of a broad expanse of muscular chest beneath faded sky-blue cotton, not to mention a healthy set of biceps. Just what she needed, a great set of biceps…to fix the fridge, of course.

Clearing her throat, she said, 'It's been flat out here. I haven't had a moment's peace.'

His right eyebrow rose a fraction, as if questioning her rather pathetic excuse for not calling him. 'Yeah, work gets like that sometimes.'

Didn't anything ever rattle him? She'd expected him to call her on her excuse, not agree with her!

'Sounded like you were busy earlier when I rang? All that noise in the background?'

Though eager to get the hinge fixed so she could usher him out of here, the polite thing would be to make a bit of small talk before offering him a coffee then the door.

'Yeah, the current project is coming along nicely.'

'Bet you still get a buzz constructing something from the ground up, getting your hands dirty.'

Her gaze drifted to his hands casually clutching the bar, and languid heat stole through her body at the thought of those strong, elongated fingers and broad palms getting downright dirty with her.

Fighting a blush, and losing, she tore her gaze away and forced it upwards, not surprised to see the glint of amusement in his eyes, and his lips curved into a knowing smile.

'I like it.'

He pushed off the bar and crossed the short space between them in a second, sending her pulse rate soaring.

She swallowed, trapped between the espresso machine and a cake display, unable to stop thinking about those hands reaching out to her, resting gently on her waist, pulling her closer and…

'Would you like me to get started?'

Her gaze flew to his as her tongue darted out to moisten her lips, her body in total meltdown.

He was talking about the fridge hinge.

Of course he was, but it didn't stop her imagination taking flight in all sorts of wicked ways as to how he could get started—with her.

'It's down here,' she managed to say, thankful her voice wasn't half as shaky as her resolve to hold him at arm's-length.

'Okay, let's take a look.'

He squatted down, dispelling the intimate fog that had surrounded them a second earlier. However, Blaine focusing his concentration on the hinge didn't help cool her down, not one bit, considering his crouching down on his haunches only served to pull the work-worn denim taut across his butt, and she stifled a groan.

Had he grown oblivious to the attraction zinging between them? Had her disinterest in returning his call served its purpose? If so, she should be springing over the bar and adding a high side-kick for good measure. Instead, she squatted down next to him, disgruntled and confused and totally out of sorts.

It had been so long since she'd felt this way, preferring to play it safe where guys were concerned and not date, knowing she could rely on her business—the male of the species another matter.

Right now, staring at Blane's butt with heat licking along her veins and sending her intentions to hold him at bay up in smoke, safe was the furthest thing from her mind.

'I assumed you have tools when you said you'd given it a go yourself at trying to fix this?'

'Uh-huh.'

Reaching under the nearby bench, she pulled out her tool kit and slid it over to him.

'It's pink.'

'Your powers of observation are truly amazing,' she said, biting the inside of her cheek to stop herself from joining in his laughter.

'I've never seen a pink toolbox before.'

She rolled her eyes and flipped it open, handing him the screwdriver he'd need.

'That's because you work with boys. I'm sure if you had the foresight to hire a woman to be on your work crew, you'd see pink tool kits every day of the week.'

'Maybe.'

He grinned as he took the proffered screwdriver, his fingers brushing hers, sending shards of electricity shooting up her arm as she struggled not to yank her hand back. 'I'm impressed.'

'With the pink tool kit?'

He glanced at her out of the corner of his eye, his mouth twitching. 'With the fact you knew which screwdriver to use.'

Puffing up like a true feminist, she said, 'I'm not a helpless female. I know a Phillips head from a flathead.'

'Obviously.'

She knew he was baiting her, teasing her as he had too many times to recall when they'd first met, and it felt good. It felt downright fantastic to be firing right back at him, to be swapping banter without guarding her words for fear of saying the wrong thing.

'Think you can extend those tool-discriminating skills to hand me a wrench?'

'Here you go, wise guy.'

She handed him the wrench, being careful to keep her fingers out of contact this time, and releasing a tiny sigh of disappointment when it worked.

For someone who knew her mind, went out and grabbed life with both hands, giving it a good shake-up along the way, she couldn't believe how contrary he made her feel. She was wavering and vacillating all over the place, wishing for one thing, hoping for another.

If she wasn't careful, she'd find herself agreeing to spend a little time with him…and they both knew exactly where that would lead.

Directly to matrimonial trouble.

With a soft grunt, he muttered, 'Almost there,' and she rued the fact considering she'd been enjoying the display of bulging biceps as he held the wrench steady, his back muscles shifting under his T-shirt as he turned the screwdriver with his other hand.

'Got it.'

With a final twist of the screwdriver, he

straightened, and she dragged her eyes upward with regret.

She'd got it all right—got it bad for her husband, who'd breezed into her life when she'd least expected or wanted it.

'Thanks. I wouldn't have had a hope of fixing it myself, would I?'

He smiled and handed her back the tools. 'You did great—it had bent out of shape a tad and needed a bit of muscle power to get it back into alignment.' He winked as he flexed his arm to display the said muscle. 'Glad I could oblige.'

'Uh-huh,' she mumbled, unable to drag her gaze away from the muscle play in his upper arm, the yearning she'd managed to dampen flaring in a second.

'Want a coffee?' she blurted, springing up from her haunches like a jack-in-the-box, needing the safety of doing a routine, everyday activity to steady her shredded resolve.

She'd made a decision not to contact him, closely followed by a need to search out those old divorce papers and put an end to this once and for all. But now she'd seen him again in the flesh—so to speak—her intentions were shot.

The sparks resurrected between them the other night were still there, had intensified if anything, and with a little fanning could burst into a raging inferno of mutual passion, the type of passion she'd only ever had with this one special guy.

'I'd love one, thanks.'

Grateful she had her back turned so he couldn't see her scorching cheeks, she tried to concentrate on operating the machine, letting out an almighty yell when he sneaked up behind her and placed his hands on her waist.

'Are you okay?'

'Apart from the fact you just scared me half to death?'

She whirled to face him, her unjustified indignation melting away as she looked into his eyes, the desire she glimpsed taking her breath away.

'You seem jumpy.'

With his hands burning a hole through her flimsy silk top, the smell of cedar enveloping her in a heady cloud and making her wish she could work outdoors right alongside him, she tilted her chin up, willing her arms to stay by her sides and not reach up and slide around his waist.

'Just tired.'

It sounded like the pathetic excuse it was.

'You sure that's all it is?'

What could she say? That he had her so physically aware of him she was tied up in knots?

That she'd barely slept all week for dreaming of him? Remembering how good it had been between them? Wishing it could be again? Yet knowing it could never be, not with her infertility an ever-present shadow looming over her, no matter how much she'd come to terms with it herself.

'Uh-huh.'

She took a step back, leaving him no option but to drop his hands.

'Espresso? Or would you like me to whip you up one of our signature coffees? I make a mean café latte fredo.'

Thankfully, he bought her distraction. 'What's in it?'

'One part espresso, five parts cold milk, shaken with ice.'

'Done.'

He stepped back, giving her room to move, and she grabbed the cocktail shaker, scooped in the ice, and set about making the coffee in record time so she could re-establish some kind of equilibrium.

'What's that you're having?'

'A doppio. Double shot of espresso.' As if she needed to stay awake all night again. 'So what do I owe you?'

'Nothing.'

Her hand stilled on the espresso machine, and she sent him her best 'don't mess with me' glare.

'I have to pay you. It's only fair.'

'Payment, huh?'

She didn't like the gleam in his eyes or the cunning smile spreading across his face. Both could give a girl ideas—very naughty ideas.

'Fine. My payment is dinner.'

Oh, no. No, no, no.

Dinner would involve sitting across from him, staring into those intriguing grey eyes, seeing them crinkle every time he smiled—which was way too often—and trying not to fall under his spell.

Blane was charm personified, and if seeing

him for barely thirty minutes had her in this much of a dither, what hope would she have of spending an entire evening with him and coming out unscathed, resolve intact, at the end of it?

'I'd rather just pay you.'

She busied herself with making the coffee, injecting the right amount of nonchalance into her voice, hoping he'd accept her subtle brush-off.

'It's dinner or I take you to the consumer affairs board for non-payment.'

'You're kidding?'

Of course he was, those adorable crinkles on full display as she sent him a look of disbelief.

He shrugged, his smile not waning. 'Maybe. Though it is a non-negotiable deal. Dinner. You and me. You choose the place, seeing as you're insisting on paying, though I have to tell you, having you shout me a meal doesn't sit well with me.'

'Why? Used to being the macho male, huh?'

'Used to being the polite male who likes to treat his wife right.'

His low, husky tone left her in little doubt as to

how well he would treat her, and in that instant she made one of those split-second decisions she'd probably regret later but couldn't resist now.

'Okay, dinner it is.'

'Great. Tomorrow night suit?'

She opened her mouth to fob him off with some lame excuse about checking her diary, before snapping it shut.

He'd been nothing but helpful, courteous and lovely to her, and if all he expected in return was dinner, she'd be churlish not to oblige.

Who was she kidding? Dinner wasn't all he was expecting—far from it. He wanted her, as his *wife*, a concept fast losing its initial lack of appeal.

'Sounds good.'

She picked up the cocktail shaker and shook it as if her life depended on it, the jumbled contents whirling around in similar fashion to her chaotic emotions.

Accepting his offer had her torn between dancing through the café while singing out loud and running to the storeroom out back to hide for the next month.

'Are you going to pick me up?'

His teasing smile warmed her heart as she poured his coffee into a tall glass and handed it to him.

'Thought we'd already got past that point the other night?'

He laughed and raised his glass to her. 'I didn't pick you up. I asked my wife out.'

There he went again with the wife thing.

Okay, so he was right; technically she was still his wife, but that was all it was, a technicality. A fact that could be easily remedied, would be easily remedied if he'd stop smiling at her for two seconds so she could muster her resolve to not let him back in her life again.

Feigning a nonchalance she didn't feel, she shrugged. 'Same diff.'

Taking a sip, he sighed his appreciation. 'You're splitting hairs. Or should that be coffee beans?'

Laughing, she sipped her doppio, savouring the strong, hot rush of caffeine. 'Fine. I'll swing by your place. Make this a real equal-opportunity dinner date.'

'Nothing sexier than a chivalrous woman.'

He winked and her heart turned over, beating a hundred miles a minute as she sent him a tremulous smile which hopefully covered the fact she was a quivering mess of nerves inside.

He thought she was sexy.

He was flirting with her in a light, non-pressured, appealing kind of way.

He was throwing everything at her defences, weakening her determination to hold him at bay with every seductive smile, with every twinkle in his gorgeous grey eyes.

It would be so easy to give in, so tempting to see how good they could be together now they were older, wiser, more mature.

But was she willing to take the risk? For there was nothing surer than the more time she spent with Blane the more likely it was that she would fall for him all over again, every charming inch.

Surely she couldn't tread down the marriage road again? Not when it would involve baring her soul about the one thing she'd buried deep inside, her gut-wrenching sorrow at not being able to have children buried with the yearning for a baby she never knew she'd had until the option had been ripped away from her.

'So now we've got that worked out, is it safe to bring up the topic of your project manager?'

'All sorted.'

She dropped her gaze to her doppio before he could read her desperation. Yet another builder had walked this week, leaving her with a half-finished apartment and a permit that ran out shortly.

But she couldn't hire him, not when she wanted him out of her life, and once she'd paid her dues with this dinner that was it.

No more meeting up, no more pseudo-dates, no more sharing coffees and chocolate.

The thought saddened her more than she could have dreamed possible.

'Really?'

'Uh-huh.' She nodded vigorously, hoping the builder she'd lined up to meet in the morning would be exactly what she needed, for she couldn't afford any more delays on the renovations, and having Blane so ready, willing and able to help wasn't conducive to her getting him out of her life for good.

'Fair enough, but remember the offer still stands. If you need some help, I'm your man.'

I'm your man.

He'd certainly been that at one time, for those all-too-short glorious three months when they'd laughed and teased and played as if they were the only romantic couple on the planet, a time when he'd been her fabled knight in shining armour and she would have happily followed him to the ends of the earth, secure in their love.

A time for long leisurely strolls on sultry summer evenings, hand in hand, idly exchanging hopes and dreams. A time for sharing hot fudge sundaes, play-fighting over who got the cherry on top and kissing the drips of chocolate from each other's lips.

A time for newly awakened passion under starry nights, for eager caresses and soft sighs as they explored each other in intimate detail while snuggled under a picnic blanket down by the river.

But that time had long gone, faded into oblivion along with her dreams for a family, and he wasn't her man any longer, despite every cell in her body screaming to get reacquainted with her husband.

Needing to get rid of him before she did something even more stupid than agree to have dinner with him as some silly payback for services rendered, she cast a pointed glance at her watch.

'Thanks, but I'll be fine. Now, I need to lock up and get some shut-eye. Big day tomorrow.'

'No worries.'

Downing his iced coffee in a few thirsty gulps, he placed the glass in the sink behind the bar and ran the tap. 'You said you lived nearby. Want me to walk you there? I've heard there's been some trouble around here lately.'

Chuckling, she jerked a thumb over her left shoulder. 'Don't worry, I'm not walking anywhere. I'm sleeping out the back while my apartment's being renovated.'

'You're kidding?'

He shook his head, his horrified expression sending a warm glow through her. He still cared about her, even if she didn't want him to.

'There's no way you're staying here. A locksmith on a job today said almost every café and restaurant along this strip has been broken into late at night or in the early hours, and he was called out this morning to the sushi place in the next block.'

'Really?'

She hadn't heard. Then again, the Niche had been running on one speed—flat out—since she'd opened up around eight. 'Did they take much?'

Stepping closer, he laid a hand on her upper arm, his touch sending slivers of searing heat crackling through her.

'They didn't only rob the place. They knifed one of the kitchen hands who'd come in early to do some prep.'

'Oh, no!' Her hand flew to her mouth, her stomach roiling in shock at such a horrific, violent act happening so close to home. 'Was he okay?'

'It was a woman. Which is why you're not staying here on your own, no matter what you say.'

Shrugging off his hand, she squared her shoulders. 'Look, I'll be fine. I'm used to taking care of myself. And, besides, I have an alarm.'

His lips set in a thin, stubborn line. 'You don't think they had an alarm at the sushi place? Or all the other places along this precinct?'

He ran a hand through his hair, his jaw set, his exasperation palpable.

'These guys slashed that poor girl even after she'd handed over the takings; it's pretty obvious they're brazen, hardened criminals who don't give a damn about who they hurt or how badly. So there's no way you're staying here alone. Haven't you got someone you can stay with?'

'Do you think I'd be sleeping on a dodgy fold-out camp bed in the storeroom if I did?'

The sarcastic response popped out before she could think, and she mentally clamped a hand over her big mouth. Great, now he'd think she was a loser with no friends, when the truth of the matter was…well…apart from Anna, who rented a single room in a boarding house, she wasn't close to anyone.

She'd liked it that way, had fostered her independence deliberately when she'd first come to Melbourne, eager to obliterate her painful memories of Blane and her traitorous parents and the baby that would never be by burying herself in making the Niche the best darn café this city had ever seen.

She'd learned it was easier not to rely on people, for they always let you down no matter how close or how much you loved them.

'Well, then, there's only one thing for it.'

She didn't like the intent in his eyes, his rigid expression. 'You'll have to stay with me.'

'No way!'

The corners of his mouth twitched. 'Would you like some more time to think about your answer?'

Shaking her head, she backed away from him. Silly, really, as if physical distance could stop the current vibrating between them.

'Thanks for the offer, but—'

'Cam, this is non-negotiable. You're not safe here, and there isn't a hope in hell I'm taking no for an answer. You're staying with me till your renovations are done, and that's final.'

'Is it now?'

Folding her arms over her chest, she tilted her chin and glared at him, hating his high-and-mighty attitude while a small part of her couldn't help but love this new, take-charge Blane.

He'd always been so laid-back, so unruffled, and she'd loved that about him, yet this new commanding, powerful, take-no-prisoners guy was pretty impressive, too.

'Look, this doesn't have to be complicated.' He held his hands out, palms up, as if he didn't have any tricks up his sleeves. 'I'm not trying to pressure you, and this isn't some underhanded, dastardly plan to get you where I want you.'

Crossing the small space between them, he cradled her face before she could move, his touch warm and soothing and oh-so-right. 'I care about you. And if it makes you feel any better, just consider my offer as that of a friend, no strings attached, okay?'

Was he insane? No strings attached? Not only were they bound by strings, they were lassoed, hog-tied and entangled in thick unbreakable rope.

If seeing him again after all this time was hard, living under the same roof would be pure torture.

She couldn't do it.

However, she hadn't got as far as she had in the city without a healthy serving of common sense, and right now her street savvy was telling her she was taking her independent stand to extremes.

She could trust Blane, he'd always been a man of his word, and if he was offering her a safe place to stay, she'd be smart to take it.

The Niche might be her life, but she'd be stupid to risk losing hers over it.

Staring up into his eyes, the flecks glowing cobalt, she knew there was only one answer she could give him: the sensible one.

He dropped his hands as she nodded slowly. 'Okay. Thanks for the offer.'

She could have sworn he sagged with relief, and the depth of his caring struck her anew.

'Great. Ready to go?'

'Actually, I need to finalise some stuff before tomorrow, so why don't you go ahead, and I'll swing past your place later?'

'No, I'll wait.'

She laid a hand on his arm, hoping to convey her thanks at his chivalry. 'I'll be fine. It's still early. There are people everywhere, and I'll be sure to leave before dark.'

His gaze flickered to her hand, shaded and in-scrutable, before slowly rising to meet hers. 'You sure?'

She nodded. 'I'll see you soon.'

Indecision warred with stubbornness across his face as she squeezed his arm. 'Go. I promise I won't be long behind you.'

After a long moment, he covered her hand with

his. 'Ring me if you need someone to walk you out of here, okay?'

Smiling at his overprotectiveness, and feeling suitably warm and fuzzy because of it, she said, 'Okay.'

'I live in the Eureka Towers on Southbank. Apartment 8801. I'll buzz you up when you get there. Take care.'

Dropping an all-too-brief kiss on her cheek, he sent her a half-salute and walked away, leaving her with the craziest urge to run after him.

CHAPTER FOUR

CAMRYN stared at the elevator buttons in confusion.

'This can't be right,' she thought, wondering if she should pop out to the doorman and ask him to re-buzz Blane and double-check.

According to the fancy engraved writing above the gold buttons there was only one apartment, 8801, on the entire eighty-eighth floor of the swanky Eureka Towers. Only one? Considering the building was ninety-two storeys, and the eighty-eighth was the highest anyone could access, she'd hazard a guess Blane lived in the penthouse.

A penthouse which covered a whole floor?

Shaking her head in disbelief, she hit the button for 8801 and backed against the rear of the elevator, finding small comfort in the feel of hard, cold, gold-plated steel panels at her back, while her startled reflection stared back at her from surrounding mirrored glass.

Either he made an absolute fortune out of building or he was house-sitting for someone. And if so, he certainly moved in higher circles than she did.

She vaguely remembered the publicity surrounding the Towers when it first opened, about it being the tallest residential tower in the world and a penthouse costing around seven million dollars. The figure alone made her feel faint, exacerbated by the nine-second ride to the eighty-eighth floor.

Blinking as the doors soundlessly slid open, she stepped out, pulling a small wheelie suitcase, and caught her breath at the pale-gold carpets embossed with cream swirls, the filigree around the down-lights and the incredibly detailed cornices.

This place was stunning, and she hadn't even made it into his *apartment* yet.

Pressing the doorbell, she smoothed her skirt, her belly churning with nerves.

It had nothing to do with this place and everything to do with the man about to open the door, a man she couldn't stop thinking about, a man with the potential to distract her from her number one goal: to make the Niche the best café in Melbourne.

She didn't do distractions.

She couldn't afford to.

Her success in the city was the only thing that kept the loneliness demons away, kept her focused enough to not lament the loss of her husband, a possible baby and a family that had betrayed her trust in them.

As the door swung open, she fixed a smile on her face and forced her hands to her sides. If she smoothed her skirt any more it would look as if she'd spent the last hour ironing. And it was bad enough she'd decided to change without him thinking she'd gone overboard.

'Hey, Cam. Come on in.'

Easy for him to say. How was a girl supposed to walk when her knees started shaking the moment she caught sight of him in sand-coloured chinos, casual white shirt and barefoot, looking laid-back and slightly mussed and sexy all at the same time.

Willing her knees to behave—lock, lift, flex—she walked past him, his fresh-from-the-shower scent not playing fair with her poor wobbly legs.

'Nice place. Though kind of small, isn't it?'

He chuckled, took her suitcase, propped it near the door and propelled her into the monstrous lounge area with a gentle hand in her back, an innocuous touch that had no right playing havoc with her body.

'I like my space.'

'It's yours?'

She stopped at the floor-to-ceiling glass windows, her breath catching at the incredible view of Melbourne and its surrounds spread out like a fairy-tale city in the dusk.

'Yeah, I bought it off the plan when they were building this place.'

With a superhuman effort she bit her tongue to stop from blurting what she was thinking: how could he afford a place like this?

Instead, she focused on identifying landmarks, taking in the sweeping vista from the Blue Dandenongs mountain range to Port Phillip Bay, from the beautiful Botanical Gardens laid out like a lush green carpet to the sparkling waters of Albert Park Lake.

And she thought she had great views in her tenth-storey Docklands apartment!

'You're curious, aren't you?'

'About?' she returned pseudo-casually.

Gesturing to a Chippendale sofa for her to take a seat, he smiled. 'About this place.'

Sinking into the deep leather, she crossed her legs, grateful she'd gone with the mid-calf pencil skirt and not her favourite above-the-knee mini which she always slipped into after work.

'I'm a little intrigued,' she admitted.

Taking a seat next to her, he rested his arm across the back and leaned towards her.

'With me or my place?'

Overwhelmed by his nearness, she took a deep breath, his aftershave filtering through her senses, the intoxicating scent of pure Blane encouraging her to bridge the short gap between them and bury her nose in the crook of his neck. Right on the tempting spot where his collar rested against his neck, where his impressive tan dipped away to broad shoulders covered in cotton, the sensitive spot she knew for a fact would drive him wild if she nipped it.

She could lie, pretend there was nothing between them, act as if he didn't affect her one little bit. But that wouldn't be fair to either of them, and they'd been through too much to start playing games now.

'Both,' she said, tilting her chin up to meet his gaze head on, challenging him to…what?

Say she intrigued him, too? That was a given considering he wanted them to have a second chance.

Tell her she was crazy for contemplating giving him what he wanted? That went without saying, for no matter how many times she evaluated this logically, her emotional side would creep up and give her a big whack over the head, urging her to go for it.

Kiss her senseless? Personally, the last option was her preferred choice, but for now she'd settle for a healthy dose of honesty, starting with how he came to afford a place like this.

Cupping her chin, he brushed a thumb along her jaw, sending shivers of longing through her.

'Careful. Your new flatmate might go getting ideas if you say he intrigues you.'

Disconcerted by his unwavering stare, she aimed for light-hearted, anything to quell the urge to shove his hand away before she did something crazy like hang on to it for dear life.

'So, tell me how you got this place. Let me guess. You've given up building to be a drug lord.'

'No.'

'You've discovered you're the secret love child of Bill Gates?'

His mouth twitched. 'No.'

'Well, come on then, spill it.'

With a slow, sexy grin that did wicked things to her heart rate, he said, 'We didn't exactly get around to discussing my job the other night or earlier this evening, did we?'

'That would be because you were too busy playing the burly builder.'

She smiled, wondering if he'd remember how she used to call him that, how she'd teased him mercilessly.

His eyes narrowed, losing none of their sparkle.

'Playing, huh? Just for the record, we're all grown up now, in case you haven't noticed.'

Oh, she'd noticed all right; as her belly dropped in a frightening free fall, her core temperature ratcheted up by about a hundred degrees, and she itched to bridge the gap between them and clamber onto his lap.

See, she knew this cohabiting thing was a bad idea.

She'd barely made it through the front door, and already her imagination was overreacting while her body...well, needless to say, her body needed some attention, something she would definitely not be getting from Blane if she knew what was good for her.

'Okay, so tell me about this building job of yours,' she said, opting for a nice, safe answer, something that wouldn't give him the opportunity to flirt considering she desperately needed a few moments to compose herself and stop thinking about exactly how he'd grown up.

'Ever heard of BA Constructions?'

She shook her head, the name vaguely familiar, the type of thing she might have seen on billboards or scaffolding around the city. 'Not sure.'

'That's my company.'

He pronounced it with the kind of unaffected casualness she'd come to associate with him from the first minute he'd bowled into her parents' old-fashioned coffee shop and swept her off her feet, the quiet confidence of a guy who knew what he wanted and how to get it.

'Tell me about it.'

'The Melbourne Cricket Ground renovation? We were contracted to do it.'

Just like that, the proverbial penny dropped. BA Constructions wasn't just any company; they'd made headlines for securing the megadeal to renovate Melbourne's biggest sports stadium ahead of larger, more established construction companies. And there'd been something about making a financial magazine's rich list, too...

'BA Constructions, huh? Blane Andrews, CEO extraordinaire by the sounds of things.'

He shrugged, his self-deprecating smile adorable. 'You know I'm basically a builder at heart. I worked hard, got the right contacts, put in the hard yards and it paid off.'

And how, if this swanky penthouse was any indication.

'I'm happy for you,' she said, instinctively reaching out to touch his hand, proud beyond belief he'd achieved so much.

'Thanks. I did it for us.'

Heat infused his gaze, instant and smouldering, burning her with its intensity, drawing her to him like a moth to a scorching flame: hypnotic, inevitable, despite the struggle to escape.

'Because I wanted to come back to you with something we can build a future on. A strong foundation for what I hope we can achieve together. You know that, right?'

She nodded reluctantly, wishing she could leap off the sofa and put some much-needed distance between them, but unable to move, caught up in something bigger and more powerful than the both of them.

Capturing her hand, he brushed his thumb across the back of it, soft, gentle caresses which sent heat spiralling out of control through her.

'I know I said no pressure, and, believe me, I intend to stick to it, but I need you to tell me exactly what you're thinking about all of this. About us.'

There is no us popped into her head, though thankfully she had the foresight not to blurt it out despite her befuddled brain as his thumb continued to do its thing.

She'd already waged an inner battle for the last few hours, dreaming up ways to pull out of staying here while secretly looking forward to it, devising ways to ditch their dinner date while ensuring she paid her debt.

He had her confused, bamboozled and hotter than she'd ever been. And she was tired of pretending this all meant nothing, that he could breeze into her life without affecting her.

Sighing, she turned her hand over, sliding her fingers between his, the intertwining sending a feeling of simple joy through her.

This was some of the stuff she'd missed about being part of a couple: the hand-holding, the shared moments, the in-jokes.

Maybe she could get to know him a little better, get reacquainted, see where it led. What did she have to lose, when she'd lost the most important thing—him—years earlier?

'You want to know what I think? I think you're crazy for waltzing back into my life and thinking we can pick up where we left off.'

A slight frown appeared between his brows, and she raised a finger to it, tenderly smoothing it away. 'But I also think you're interesting, funny and pretty cute. After all this time, go figure.'

His eyes sparked with delight, and she laughed. 'I also think seeing as you've been kind enough to let me crash here for a bit, it's only fair I cut you some slack.'

His answering smile could have lit up the whole of Melbourne. 'I like the way you think.'

To prove it, he closed the short gap between them and kissed her.

Fireworks exploded in her head. Heat raced through her body. And the shield around her heart thawed and cracked as she recognised on an instinctive level that this kiss meant more than she could have possibly imagined.

She'd fooled herself into thinking she hadn't

missed him all these years. She'd been wrong. So wrong.

This was much more than a kiss, this timeless melding of two souls meant to be together, a kiss filled with hope and new beginnings. Gentle yet forceful, giving yet demanding, he kissed her with a precision that took her breath away.

As he cradled her head, his lips grazing hers with slow, seductive skill, she knew the explosion of mind-numbing need flowing through her had little to do with expertise and everything to do with the potent attraction still simmering between them after all this time.

They'd always been like this together. Lightning-fast, combustible sparks shooting between them: quick, hot, magical.

'You're smiling.' He broke the kiss to pull back and look at her. 'Either it means you're really happy or my kissing technique needs a bit of work.'

Reaching up to lay a hand against his cheek, she smiled. 'Your kissing technique is as good as ever.'

'Okay, then, glad we got that sorted.'

His confident grin told her he knew exactly

how talented he was in the kissing department and had probably been fishing for compliments.

'You shaved.' She ran her fingertips over his jaw, skimming the smooth skin, irrationally missing the stubble she loved so much.

'You know it's a lost cause. I'll have half a beard again by the end of the night.'

'I like it,' she murmured, replacing her fingertips with her lips, grazing his cheek in the lightest, barest of kisses, inhaling deeply as she did so, her memory dancing with joy in recognition of his fresh, addictive scent.

'You still have the power to drive me crazy.'

He turned his head a fraction to slant his mouth across hers in a slow, soul-drugging kiss that had her clinging to his shirt as if she was floundering out of her depth in a sea of desire.

'So what are you going to do about it?'

She broke the kiss with reluctance, her body telling her to go for it, her head telling her to take things slowly before they got in too deep too quickly.

'How about we take it each day at a time?'

'Each day, huh?'

Wriggling back on the sofa to put a little distance between them—she couldn't think straight with his overpowering masculine presence in her personal space—she decided to give it to him straight.

'I don't want you to think me moving in here is agreeing to give us another chance. I'm not ready for that, I'm not sure if I'll ever be ready. I understand your rationale for leaving, but that doesn't mean I agree with it or what it did to us. You did what you thought was right at the time, but everything has changed now. I've changed…' If he only knew how…

She shook her head, trying to read the expression on his face, coming up empty. 'So if you're happy to hang out as friends while I'm here that's fine, but I'm not making any promises, okay?'

Something dark and mysterious shifted in his eyes before they crinkled at the corners, his smile a welcome sign he didn't think she was completely batty.

'Phew, that was some speech you just made. Don't hold back or anything, will you?'

'You know blunt is my middle name.'

'Honesty is good,' he said, but as his gaze dipped to where they held hands, she knew he was hiding something.

She'd worked in the hospitality industry her whole life, first in her parents' coffee shop in Rainbow Creek, now in the Niche, and if there was one skill she'd developed besides making a great latte it was reading people.

Since he'd strolled into the Niche, he'd been nothing but open and straightforward, always meeting her eye, so what was with the sudden shift? Guess she'd soon find out, considering she'd agreed to live with him till her apartment was done.

Sheer and utter madness, yet she hadn't felt this alive in a long, long time.

'So you want to hang out with me, huh?'

His eyes gleamed with anticipation and she wondered if she'd imagined the whole evasion thing a second ago.

Tilting her chin, she flicked her hair over her shoulder, delighting in his tortured expression. 'Absolutely.'

Leaning closer, he dropped his voice to a conspiratorial whisper and crooked his finger at her. 'Well, here's a thought.'

Smiling, she cupped a hand around her ear. 'I'm listening.'

'How about a date?'

'Friends don't date. And, besides, you're pushing your luck, seeing as I'm already taking you to dinner.'

He laughed and capturing her hand, dragged it away from her ear to place a soft, hot kiss on her palm. The urge to curl her fingers over it was beyond tempting.

'Dinner's about this strong-willed woman demanding she pay me for services rendered. So, the way I see it, a date has the potential to be something else entirely.'

She gulped as a sizzle of anticipation licked along her veins, her pulse picking up speed in pace with her hopes.

Blane had the potential to light up her life again, to give her the buzz she'd been craving since he'd walked out a lifetime ago.

So why was she hesitating?

Kids.

It always came down to her inability to conceive and the ramifications of what that might have on any relationship she'd be foolish enough to enter. Though there was more to it this time, and she knew it.

Was it possible that, deep down, she knew letting him into her life for any length of time could tempt her to want more? Maybe have a marriage for real this time, despite what she couldn't give him?

The thought terrified her, and her stomach backflipped with dread that she might be silly enough to make the same mistake twice.

But she wasn't silly. She wasn't the same person anymore. This time, maybe she'd get to have her tiramisu and eat it, too.

Leaping up from the sofa, she pulled him up with her. 'Come on, let's go have that dinner I owe you.'

He laughed. 'Why the rush?'

'The sooner we eat the sooner you get to convince me why I should let you take me out on a date.'

Smiling, he picked her up and whirled her around, and she flung her head back and laughed, relishing this amazing, carefree feeling.

He'd done the same thing when she'd agreed to marry him, though back then he'd spun her around so fast and for so long they'd both tumbled onto the cushiony moss at the foot of the old cedar tree, breathless and laughing and kissing, enchanted by the moment, so wrapped up in each other the world around them had ceased to exist.

He'd been her everything…before vanishing into nothing, and she'd be foolish to forget that, no matter how good it felt to laugh with him again.

He stopped, and she slid down his body, slowly and deliberately, soft cotton slithering against smooth silk, her skin tingling, yearning for full body contact, the shift from playful to lustful clear as his gaze riveted to hers.

'How about next weekend for this date I'm going to persuade you to go on?'

'I do the rosters quarterly, so I'm tied up every weekend for the next three months. The earliest weekend I'm free is June.'

'That should give you plenty of time to get used to the idea.'

'If you convince me, that is,' she said, giving

in to an impulsive, crazy urge to entwine her hands around his neck and drag his head down for a swift, passionate kiss, pulling away before she found herself in bed with him *before* the first date. Though technically that was probably allowed, considering it wouldn't be the first time for either of them! 'And believe me, I'm going to be a very hard sell.'

Resting his forehead against hers, he murmured, 'I think you know how persuasive I can be,' before stepping away, offering her his hand and gesturing towards the door with the other.

As she slipped her hand into his, Camryn knew whatever he had in store for her, she didn't stand a chance of refusing.

CHAPTER FIVE

CAMRYN sighed with relief as she sank into the plush suede sofa, curled her legs under her, and propped the giant plastic bowl filled with popcorn on her lap.

It had been too long since she'd had a night off, let alone the freedom to watch a chick-flick, and, what with Blane called out for an emergency meeting, this had been too good an opportunity to pass up.

Not that he hadn't made her feel welcome or not told her to make herself at home. In fact, he'd gone out of his way to ensure she treated the penthouse as her own for however long she needed to be here.

Not long, if she had any say it.

Quite simply, living with Blane was pure and utter torture. Oh, not in the rooming sense, for he was the perfect housemate: own bathroom, clean kitchen, stocked fridge where he didn't touch her stuff, toilet seat always thoughtfully down.

Throw in the fact he respected her privacy, didn't expect her to make small talk in the morning when she was at her grumpiest, and didn't hound her for leaving a trail of magazines around the place, and he was nigh on perfect in her eyes.

But therein lay the problem.

Blane *was* perfect, from the top of his mussed hair to the bottom of his sexy bare feet as he padded from his bedroom to the kitchen in the middle of the night for a drink of water.

She'd lie awake in bed, listening to his soft footfall against the polished boards, holding her breath as he passed her room, the small, traitorous part of her wishing he'd enter on some flimsy excuse.

Pathetic.

Considering she'd been the one to reinforce the 'just friends' mantra when she moved in, it was rather ironic she was having the most difficulty sticking to it.

She'd see him first thing in the morning, his jaw covered in stubble, and want to caress his cheek. She'd smell him fresh out of the shower as he left a fragrant cloud of steam in his wake as she walked past the bathroom door and will herself not to inhale deep lungfuls of the heady stuff.

She'd hear him humming softly to himself as he got dressed and try to blot out the vivid mental image that sprang to mind of what he looked like without clothes.

Shaking her head, she stuffed a handful of popcorn in her mouth and hit Play on the remote. She needed to chill-out with this romantic comedy, have a few laughs, and forget about Blane for two hours.

However, like most of her plans these days, they didn't run smoothly, and as the opening credits rolled onto the screen, she heard the front door swing open.

'Hey, there. What are you watching?'

Her heart galloped as he plopped onto the couch beside her, looking wind-tossed and deliciously dishevelled in his rumpled tan T-shirt and faded denim, resident smile in place.

'Some girly movie Anna recommended to me about three years ago.'

He laughed. 'Don't get much time to watch DVDs, huh?'

'Try never.'

'Mind if I watch it with you?'

Great. She'd look like a churlish cow if she refused, but what happened to her Blane-free time? Not only would she be forced to sit through one hundred and twenty minutes of having him less than three feet away, she could actually smell him, the faintest waft of cedar instantly transporting her back to a time she shouldn't be remembering let alone craving.

'What are you thinking?'

Her gaze flew to his, her breath catching at the tenderness she glimpsed there, and, while it would be smarter to fob him off, she was too caught up in the moment to lie.

'Remember that old cedar tree?'

His eyes crinkled, his smile warm. 'The one with the old tyre? Sure. You used to love playing princess, ordering me around like some lowly serf to push you for ages.'

She chuckled at the memory, catapulted back to a time where they had nothing better to do than tease each other, laugh with each other, at total ease, secure in their love.

What she wouldn't give for a step back in time.

'There were times you used to order me around, like when we used to walk miles through the National Park on the outskirts of town.'

'Yeah.' His eyes twinkled with amusement. 'Though you made me haul a ten-tonne picnic on my back every time.'

'That's because you were always starving.'

The minute the words popped out of her mouth, his eyes darkened to smoky grey, and she knew in an instant he was thinking of other appetites beside food.

'Speaking of being starving, here, have some popcorn.'

She shoved the bowl towards him, not surprised her hand trembled.

He had that effect on her, always had, and she clamped her lips together to refrain from saying anything else she might regret.

'Thanks.'

He tossed a few kernels up in the air, tilted his head back, and caught them as they dropped into his mouth, like he'd always done, and, once again, she was transported back in time, to the weekly movie sessions at the town hall where they'd sat in the back stalls, holding hands so tightly her fingers had tingled, her head resting on his shoulder, snuggling into his warmth.

Those had been good times, amazing times, and for those magical three months he'd held her spellbound, caught up in a whirlwind of passion and laughter and friendship the likes of which she'd never known.

But he'd left, leaving a gaping hole in her life, a soul-deep emptiness which haunted her to this day, and, while she'd accepted his rationale for leaving, it didn't mean she had a desire to go back there again.

A good, sound decision. If only her body would agree, and sitting this close to him was doing serious damage to her equilibrium.

Faking a yawn, she stretched. 'Actually, I think I'm pretty beat. I might give the movie a miss.'

He was on to her.

She could see it in the slight narrowing of his eyes, the uncharacteristic downturn of his beautiful mouth.

'Cam, you can't go on avoiding me for ever. We live in the same apartment, and I rarely see you.'

Reaching out, he covered her hand with his where it rested on the sofa, and she struggled not to snatch it away.

His touch on top of her wavering hormones was not a good combination, oh, no sirree.

'What happened to hanging out as friends? Surely we can do that?'

'Of course,' she murmured, clamping down on the strongest urge to turn her hand palm up and intertwine her fingers with his. 'I've just been super-busy, that's all.'

He could have pushed the issue, made her confront the truth, but he was too much of a nice guy, and she knew it.

Giving a gentle tug on her hand, leaving her no option but to lean towards him, he said, 'So you're not running scared?'

'Of what?'

Releasing her hand to slide his palm up her arm

in a slow, sensuous caress, he bridged the short distance between them to whisper in her ear, 'Us.'

One tiny syllable with so many connotations.

Us, as in the giddy, impulsive, head-over-heels-in-love youngsters they'd been? Or us, as in the older, wiser, more mature people they'd become?

It was the latter that scared her the most, for she'd loved Blane, a twenty-one-year-old struggling tradesman with a thirst for adventure, so what hope did she have of not falling for the sexier, more together version?

She didn't move, savouring the sensation of his breath fanning against her cheek before he pulled away and released her arm, every cell in her body on high alert, crying out for more.

'Let me guess. You're going to say there is no us.'

His voice was tinged with amusement rather than rancour, and she found her mouth twitching despite the urge to deny, deny, deny just as he'd anticipated.

Shrugging, she toyed with a stray popcorn kernel that lay in her lap. 'We're friends, so that's an "us" of sorts.'

'Friends. Right.'

He didn't believe her. He knew she was a

fraud. That with every passing day it was getting harder and harder not to fall under his spell all over again.

Pushing to his feet, he rubbed his hands together as if concocting some grand Machiavellian scheme.

'Then you won't object to catching up as *friends* this weekend. After all, it's your first weekend off in months, and I've been very patient and—'

'Okay, okay, you've made your point.' Grateful he'd put some much-needed distance between their bodies, she tilted her head to look up at him. 'What did you have in mind?'

Thrusting his hands in his pockets, resulting in an eye-catching display of soft cotton pulled taut across his broad shoulders, he winked.

'Leave it to me. Whatever I come up with, rest assured, it'll be mighty friendly.'

Unable to stop a rueful smile spreading across her face, she watched him stride out of the room, wondering what on earth she'd got herself into now.

* * *

Blane stared at Cam as she dismounted the jet ski, the expanding tightness in his chest scaring the hell out of him.

He couldn't be having a heart attack. He'd had his annual physical last month, and the doctor had pronounced him fit and healthy for the average twenty-seven-year-old that had spent the bulk of his life doing manual labour before trading his tools for a desk.

If his ticker was fine, the tension in the vicinity of his heart could only mean one thing. His love for his wife was expanding and growing with each passing day.

He'd never believed in the corny love-at-first-sight thing till he'd walked into that old-fashioned rundown coffee shop in Rainbow Creek, taken one look at the spiky-haired rebel with a cheeky smile and flashing cinnamon-coloured eyes serving behind the counter, and he'd been a goner. Drifting through Victoria from town to town had suited him just fine until he'd fallen head over heels for the sassy brunette with a smile that could light up a room.

Eloping might have been impulsive, reckless

and downright stupid considering their age and how long they'd known each other, but he'd never regretted it, not one single day. The only thing he regretted was walking away from her, despite having her best interests at heart.

But he was through with regrets. This time, he'd give it all he had. Their marriage was worth it. *She* was worth it.

Oblivious to the depth of his feelings, she sent him a jaunty wave while standing in the shallows before leaning forward, twisting her hair into a tight spiral, and squeezing the water out, the sun highlighting the honey streaks in the dark molasses, creating a halo effect as she shook it out and ruffled it dry.

Halo? She was no angel that was for sure, with the constant teasing glances, the flirtatious banter, the subtle touching. Friends, she'd said. Ha! She'd been driving him crazy ever since she'd moved in, stoking his fire till he could barely think straight let alone put the finishing touches on the surprise he had lined up for her.

He'd anticipated she wouldn't want a bar of him after he'd done a runner six years ago, and he hoped the surprise would go some way to proving how seriously committed he was to reviving their marriage.

While she might be singing the 'let's take it one day at a time' tune, she was warm and spontaneous and fun as always, her actions speaking much louder than her words.

She could call their living arrangements 'hanging out together', but from where he stood they were testing the marriage waters and, while his sexy sceptical wife might be dipping her toes, he was ready to dive in the deep end.

Watching her jog across the sand towards him, he silently thanked whoever had invented wetsuits. The material outlined every gorgeous curve of her body. She'd filled out and then some since he'd first fallen in love with her, and her new figure had him craving his luscious wife more than ever.

Leaping to his feet, and dusting off his butt as she reached him, he thrust his hands into his pockets to stop himself from grabbing her and never letting go.

'So, how does this rate as a date?'

'Technically, it isn't a date. You gave me some

lame excuse about your penthouse needing to be fumigated, and I pretended to buy into it. Apparently we had to take refuge in your mate's holiday house for the weekend or suffer dire consequences from inhaling pesticides. So, really, this isn't a date, it's a necessity for my delicate constitution, right?'

He snorted. 'Delicate? Yeah, as an angle grinder.'

Chuckling, she squeezed the last droplets from the ends of her hair. 'But just so you know, I've never jet-skied before, and it's awesome.'

Her eyes glittered with pleasure as she fiddled with the zip on her wetsuit, sending his excitement meter off the scale. 'Glad you liked it.'

Seeing her like this, exuberant and glowing, resurrected the scary tight-chest feeling. Yes, they'd only just met up again. Yes, it was too early to be thinking long-term. But he knew.

Their marriage was alive and kicking.

He trusted his gut instincts, the same instincts that had made him a fortune in the building industry, the same instincts that had catapulted him to the top of the construction world and made him a multi-millionaire ten times over, and right now his gut was telling him she wanted to reunite as much as he did.

Getting reacquainted as friends was the first step, and this amazing woman, standing in the sun like some golden glowing glamazon, would hopefully be right alongside him as they took the rest of the steps towards a long, happy life together.

'You hungry yet?'

Her stomach growled in response, and she laughed, patting her belly. 'I guess falling off that thing a hundred times worked up an appetite.'

'I only counted fifty.'

Dodging the playful slap she aimed his way, he held out his hand. 'Come on. Let's head back to the car.'

She didn't hesitate, slipping her hand into his, and as he curled his fingers around hers he marvelled at how right it still felt after all this time.

Oh, yeah, she might be singing the anti-marriage tune, but this maestro had every intention of conducting them straight into a happily-ever-after concerto.

'Is there anywhere to change around here?'

He shook his head. 'Sorry. It's behind the car door or wait till we get to the house.'

The corners of her mouth curved into a deliciously naughty smile. 'Or you could hold a towel up for me, but only if you promise not to peek.'

As all the blood from his brain rushed south, he tugged on her hand till she stood flush against him, murmuring in her ear, 'No deal. And it's no use asking me to turn around because I've got eyes in the back of my head.'

'It can't be too hard, right?'

She wriggled within the circle of his arm around her waist, the wetsuit soaking water through his T-shirt, the damp a welcome relief for his skin burning up from the inside out.

'I think you know exactly how hard it is.'

He could have shown her if he shifted his pelvis a fraction to the left, but she was driving him beyond the limits any red-blooded male in his right mind could tolerate, so he settled for a quick, blistering kiss, chuckling when she gasped after he released her, and twirled her towards the car, giving her a gentle pat on her very cute butt for good measure.

'I'll give you two minutes to change. You take any longer, and I won't be responsible for my actions.'

She flung a saucy look over her shoulder. 'Is that a threat or a promise?'

'Change!' He pointed to the car before his good intentions to romance her in the style she deserved went up in flames along with his libido.

'I'll be over that sand dune.' He held up two fingers. 'Two minutes, that's it.'

With a fake pout, she puffed out an exaggerated sigh before reaching for the zip and slowly, agonisingly, drawing it downwards inch by excruciating inch.

He stood rooted to the spot, unable to tear his gaze away from her fingertips, the nails short, practical and unadorned, wrapped around that tiny piece of black metal, sliding downwards in a deliberate, unhurried tease.

She reached the tantalising dip between her breasts, the hint of cleavage making him grit his teeth to stop himself from groaning.

'Remember that time we went skinny-dipping after the Labour Day picnic?'

Remember? How could he forget? Instant memories swamped him: sharing hot nachos down by the creek, licking the spicy salsa off each other's fingers, flickering moonlight playing over her exquisite features, him daring her to join him in the frigid water, buck naked...

'Cam...' He took a step towards her, barely managing to stop when she waggled a finger at him and pointed over his shoulder.

'I think there's a sand dune over there with your name written all over it.'

With a frustrated growl, he turned away from her teasing grin and marched over the hot sand, putting as much distance between the gorgeous temptress and himself as possible.

He might be a romantic but he wasn't a saint, and if that zip had gone any further, he couldn't have been held accountable for his actions.

Cam might like to tease him, to push things along but he had all the time in the world.

Like for ever.

Camryn wondered if she'd made a mistake.

When Blane drove through the tiny coastal

town of Barwon Heads on their way back for lunch with its single main street dotted with a bakery, pub, grocer and a few cafés for the holidaymakers who probably frequented the quiet town in the summer, she'd had the distinct feeling he was trying to recapture their past.

The streets had been almost deserted, the foreshore home to a few seagulls too lazy to raise a squawk, and as the car had stopped at the lone roundabout to let a helmetless kid on a bike through, it had taken every ounce of her willpower not to interrogate him on the spot.

Barwon Heads was reminiscent of Rainbow Creek, from the few old guys loitering around the rusty anchor in the town's sole park, making desultory small talk over cigarettes, to the curious glances cast their way when Blane stopped for petrol.

And considering they'd first met in Rainbow Creek, it didn't take a genius to figure out he was trying to take a trip down memory lane.

Not a bad thing in itself when she'd enjoyed every moment she'd spent in her errant husband's company so far, and this weekend would prove no exception. The kicker lay in the fact her intentions to tread softly had flown out the window since the first time they'd kissed in his penthouse, and she hadn't been able to recover her equilibrium since.

It was getting harder and harder to hold him off, to pretend she was just getting reacquainted with a friend and not falling deeper with every passing day.

'Chardonnay or Shiraz?'

Smiling, she turned away from the wooden balcony and the panoramic view of the tiny town that lay out before them. 'Chardonnay would be lovely.'

'Coming right up.'

He tipped a finger to his head in a salute before padding back into the kitchen, his bare feet making a soft padding sound against the old wooden boards.

Sighing, she leaned against the balcony, propped on her elbows, wondering if there was such a thing as happily ever after.

Was she crazy thinking about giving their marriage a second chance after what she'd been through first time around? Considering what she'd have to tell him if she was mad enough to give in to him?

What she did know was the heady attraction zinging between them since the first moment they'd met hadn't waned. If anything it had intensified, the underlying heat needing little to burst into a raging conflagration of yearning and passion.

Not that he was pushing her, oh, no, far from it. Blane was categorically the nicest guy she'd ever met. Not to mention handsome in a rough-around-the-edges way she adored, funny, smart, thoughtful…throw in courteous, respectful, add some newly acquired chef skills to the list, and she knew she was in serious trouble.

Saying she had no interest in resurrecting their marriage was a crock, and she knew it.

To make matters worse, she'd agreed to spend the night. Not a big deal in itself, considering they'd been living together for the last month but, somehow, being housemates where they were both so busy with their respective businesses they rarely saw each other was completely different to this.

A weekend away, he'd said after she'd laughed off his fumigating excuse, time out from her busy schedule to kick back with no strings attached, and she'd foolishly agreed.

It had all seemed so simple saying yes over an espresso at the end of a long, tiring day when her body ached, her mind fogged and her soul exhausted, his offer just the thing for a workaholic who hadn't had a day off in over a year.

However, now they were here at his mate's holiday house after an incredibly fun afternoon at the beach, reality hit.

They'd be in each other's company twenty-four/seven, without the excuse of work or meetings or late-night trading to hide behind. Not that she'd been avoiding him exactly; business at the Niche had been off the scale. She'd had regular meetings with the new project manager at her apartment to ensure everything ran smoothly and on time, and some of her staff had come down with a flu bug, and she'd had to do some serious juggling.

However, it had been late at night, when she'd all but fallen into bed, that she'd been all too aware of him sleeping across the hall from her, so close…so tantalisingly close…

Now here she was, sharing meals with him, sharing memories, those precious snapshots imprinted on her brain to be flicked through at will, and the self-imposed barriers she'd erected between them would come crashing down. Then what?

She didn't stand a chance of holding him off.

'Right, here you go, one chilled Chardonnay and a seafood platter for two.'

'Thanks.'

She took the ice-cold glass from him and gulped the wine, the refreshing bite of the Hunter Valley grapes loosening her throat which had constricted at the thought of taking a risk of this magnitude.

With impeccable manners as always, he drew out a chair for her. 'You better take it easy with that stuff. If my memory serves correct, you had two sips of champers on our honeymoon night and it went straight to your head.'

'I didn't hear you complaining.'

They locked gazes, hot, smouldering, instantly transported back to a time when they'd been ecstatically happy and totally free of responsibility, a time when it had just been the two of them so wrapped up in each other they'd been ready to tackle the world head on.

But that time had passed, the opportunity for the Blane and Cam team lost.

Or was it?

He cleared his throat and took the seat opposite. 'You got that right. Those were special times, huh?'

'The best.'

The words popped out before she could think, and she grabbed her fork and speared a piece of grilled calamari, concentrating on filling her plate with the deliciously aromatic garlic prawns, salmon fillet and scallops he'd barbecued to perfection, anything to avoid blurting out any more home truths.

'Do you miss them as much as I do?'

She couldn't lie to him, couldn't hold him back for ever, and she nodded, forking a ring of butter-soft calamari into her mouth, savouring the fresh sea taste with a burst of lemon, using the scrumptious food as an excuse not to speak and betray the lump of emotion lodged in her throat.

'We could have those times again, you know.' He reached across and captured her hand, his long, warm fingers curling around hers like the most natural, comforting thing in the world. 'I think you want it as much as I do.'

This was why she shouldn't have come this weekend. A bit of light-hearted flirting she could handle, it was this revealing-your-soul thing she sucked at. And boy, would he get the shock of a lifetime when she bared her soul.

Swallowing, she washed the yummy seafood down with a sip of wine, much slower this time. 'Honestly? I don't know what I want.'

He withdrew his hand, and she raised her eyes, disheartened by the hint of wariness in his. 'That's okay. I didn't mean to get all heavy on you. This weekend's meant to be about relaxation, remember?'

The tension between them dissolved as he helped himself to seafood, but she could tell she'd hurt him. It was the last thing she wanted to do, but she had to be honest, and while they were growing closer every day, she still couldn't throw all her reservations away in one go.

'Relaxation. Right, got it,' she said, picking up her fork and twirling it between her fingers, emotions tumbling through her in a confusing torrent: fear and hope waging a fierce battle as she struggled to come to a decision. Married or not, for there would be no middle ground. She couldn't go on being friends with her husband for ever, and she didn't expect him to sit around and wait indefinitely.

She had to make a choice, and soon, for both their sakes.

Reaching for his wine glass, he raised it in her direction. 'I propose a toast. To focusing on this weekend and making it a new and exciting time to remember.'

She'd drink to that, and she picked up her glass and clinked it against his. 'To new and exciting times ahead.'

But excitement wore off. The gloss of getting reacquainted would soon fade and pale in the face of making tough decisions, the type of life-changing decisions affecting both of them once she told him the truth.

She would have to tell him about her infertility

if they were to take a second chance on their marriage; there would be no holding back despite the sick, hollow ache deep in her soul every time she thought about what she'd been through and how it affected her future...*their* future.

Excitement was fine for now. It was renewing her commitment to her husband that was confusing the heck out of her.

CHAPTER SIX

CAMRYN sank onto the threadbare rug, tucked her feet under her, and cradled a mug of hot choco-late, staring out into the inky darkness, hearing the waves crashing on the shore but unable to see anything beyond the few low-wattage street lights dotting the foreshore.

This place might be a ramshackle cottage, with its loopy wood letting in the blustery wind through tiny cracks, and its mismatched furniture and broken-spring sofa, but it held a certain appeal. Namely the man walking towards her with a plate piled high with small, symmetrical squares of caramel slice, her favourite.

'You certainly know how to spoil a gal.'

She selected a large piece, biting into the gooey caramel and coconut biscuit base and sighing. 'Mmm…good.'

She flicked her tongue out to catch a stray crumb, unwilling to let the tiniest morsel escape her lips, when her gaze collided with his, the heat she glimpsed enough to send a thrill of excitement through her.

Considering the hash she'd made over dinner, bringing up her confusion about their relationship, she was surprised Blane felt anything other than compassion for her.

But there was no mistaking the hunger in his eyes, the smouldering glow of desire she'd seen many times before and had shrugged off with a witty quip or light flirtation.

However, this time was different.

This time they were spending quality time together, more than a snatched coffee as they ran out of his penthouse in the morning or a brief greeting as they passed in the hallway heading to their respective bedrooms at night.

Here, there was no hiding behind her busy schedule, and, while he'd made it clear he didn't expect anything from this weekend beyond a bit of R&R, she knew all it would take to send them both up in flames was a little oxygen to the sparks already flying between them.

'More?'

He held out the plate towards her, his steamy gaze stoking the fire between them, and she knew he wasn't just talking about the caramel slice. Playing the nice guy, he was giving her the choice of how far she wanted to take this getting reacquainted business.

But she didn't have a choice, not really.

The second she'd lowered her defences and let this incredible man back into her life was the exact moment any choice had flown out the window, for there was nothing surer than once the two of them started spending time together again they'd end up in each other's arms. It had been a highlight of their brief relationship in Rainbow Creek, and it was still a feature now, with the constant underlying attraction between them.

Blane had been her first lover, her only lover, and it had been six long years since she'd known his exquisite touch.

The decision was a simple one as she laid a hand on his forearm, deliberately pushing the plate away as she leaned forward and breathed, 'Yes, please.'

In what seemed like an eternity, but in reality couldn't have been more than a few seconds, they shoved mugs and slice out of the way, made a frantic grab at one another and tumbled onto the rug in a flurry of tangled limbs and laughter.

'Are you sure this is what you want?'

She silenced him with a kiss, pouring all her heart and soul into it, the type of kiss which expressed more than words ever could, the type of kiss welcoming him back into her life with a resounding yes!

Lips melded, fused, clung. He tasted of chocolate and coffee, sweet, strong, addictive, and she savoured the heady rush, bunching the soft cotton of his T-shirt beneath her hands, clutching at him, needing to anchor herself in a world gone deliciously, intoxicatingly mad.

'I'll take that as a yes,' he murmured, his lips nibbling the sensitive skin behind her earlobe while his hands spanned her waist, his calloused fingertips gently rasping against her skin and sending pure, blinding desire exploding through her.

'Just take all of me.'

She could sense rather than see his smile as his

lips trailed down her neck, nuzzling the soft hollow above her collarbone.

'I like the fact my wife knows what she wants.'

His hands slid slowly upwards, grazing the underside of her breasts, and she gasped as his head suddenly dipped and he placed a hot, open-mouthed kiss on the exposed skin of her cleavage.

'Oh, I know what I want all right,' she whispered, leaning back on her hands, thrusting her breasts upwards, offering herself to him, craving more of the same all over her hypersensitised body.

He stilled, his hands cupping her breasts while he raised his head to look at her.

'Tell me.' His eyes, pewter with passion, never left hers, the heat arcing between them sending her body into meltdown. 'Tell me exactly what you want.'

Placing her palms against his rock-hard chest, she slid her hands upwards, savouring every muscular contour, relishing his matured body, her breathing coming in soft, short pants as he mimicked her action, before resting on his shoulders and giving him a gentle tug forwards.

There'd be no turning back from this.
She didn't care.
This felt right, *was* right.
'Cam?'
'I want you,' she murmured, a second before their lips touched and obliterated everything but this moment, this night, with this amazing man.

'I've got a surprise for you.'

Camryn raised an eyebrow, leaving him in little doubt she'd already loved the one he'd had for her last night. 'Another one? My, my, when you set out to impress a girl you really go all out.'

Blane laughed, the rich, mellow timbre of his chuckles raising the hair on the nape of her neck. Or maybe that had more to do with the smouldering look he gave her, the look that said he remembered exactly the mutual surprises they'd rediscovered last night, over and over.

'You're going to love this one, too.'

He ran a finger across the back of her hand as it lay on the table, the softest of caresses but enough to send heat flowing through her body. He'd touched her exactly like that all over her body last night, slow, leisurely caresses designed to tease and excite and titillate.

However, it was the way he'd emotionally touched her that had her walking around all morning with a dreamy smile on her face.

They'd made love last night, their actions far surpassing the physical act, renewing a soul-deep bond that could only exist between two people destined to be together. With every whispered endearment, with every soft embrace, he'd reawakened her love for him till she'd had no option but to recognise the truth.

She loved him. Had never stopped loving him despite steeling her heart and moving on with her life. And that truth would set her free from the mistrust and the reservations she still had. Time to move forward. Time to give them a chance, for real.

'Have you finished your sundae? We can hit the road if you have. Check out this surprise.'

She nodded, pushing away her half-eaten banana split with extra choc fudge.

Entering this small café had been like stepping back in time. Her parents' coffee shop could have been its twin. From the faded Vegemite posters on the wood-panelled walls to the blue-and-white gingham curtains, the frilly-edged threadbare cream voile tablecloths to the limited selection of hot drinks, it resembled her folks' place so much it sent a pang of nostalgia through her.

She'd even ordered her favourite childhood dessert in a pique of nostalgia, though it hadn't tasted half as good as it had back then, only serving to ram home how much she'd changed.

'I'm ready.'

She pushed away from the table and grabbed her bag, suddenly eager to escape the confines of the café. Having a sundae for old time's sake reeked of sentiment, and she didn't have time for it, not where her parents were concerned.

She'd loved them, trusted them, and they'd betrayed her. She'd wanted to believe it had all been some nasty mistake, but her mum had blurted the truth in anger and it couldn't be taken back.

She'd put all her faith in them as a good kid should. She wouldn't make the same mistake again. And she sure as hell wouldn't let thinking about them ruin this day for her.

Today was a day for celebrating how she'd re-connected with Blane last night, how making love had cemented what she'd already known.

That despite her resolve to keep this thing casual, it had evolved into more, so much more.

He wanted a real marriage? It looked like he was about to get his wish.

How many times had she dreamed about happily ever after as a teenager but only in the vague, wishful fantasy sense, envisaging the perfect guy to make all her wishes come true? Lucky for her, her fantasy had come to life and stepped into her reality—twice!—leaving her breathless and amazed and slightly shell-shocked.

It was almost too good to be true. But she was through being super-cautious. She deserved this, deserved him. Being the best café operator in Melbourne might get her noticed in the hospitality industry, but it wouldn't keep her warm at night.

Shrugging into her striped hooded top, she headed for the car, eager to see what her playful husband had in store. He was like a kid at

Christmas with this grand surprise, and she had to admit he had her revved up, too.

She propped on the front of the ute, waiting for him as he chatted to some old guy leaning against the café's striped post, using the time to absorb every impressive inch of her man.

That had a nice ring to it, *her* man, and with a smug smile she watched him rub the back of his neck in a habit of a lifetime, the simple action pulling his polo shirt up and revealing a tantalising sliver of tanned washboard abs above faded denim.

She'd explored every delicious muscular plane of his body last night, catapulted back to the past by the familiarity of it all, delightfully surprised by the newness of his adult maleness.

He'd been lean and scruffy and scrumptiously ruffled as a young man. Now her husband was an absolute dish.

After bidding the old guy goodbye with a snappy half-salute, he strode towards her, all long denim-clad legs and confidence. *Her man.* Oh, yeah, she loved the sound of that.

Swooping in for a swift kiss, he murmured

against the side of her mouth, 'That sundae must've been something else. You're practically drooling just thinking about it.'

'Who said I'm thinking about the sundae?'

Her hand slid over his hip and rested for a leisurely moment on the most tempting butt she'd ever seen, leaving him in little doubt what had put the dreamy look on her face.

He chuckled as he slung an arm over her shoulder. 'I'm flattered. But I think you're just buttering me up in an attempt to get a clue or two out of me.'

With a not-too-gentle pinch on his inspiring butt, she pulled away with mock indignation. 'I wouldn't resort to such underhandedness.'

'Yeah, you would.'

He slanted his lips over hers again as she registered she'd probably do anything to have him kiss her like this.

'Mmm…as much as I love that, I have to admit the suspense is killing me. When do I get to see this surprise?'

'Right now.'

He held the passenger door open, and she

smiled her thanks, thrilled by his impeccable manners. He'd always held doors open for her, but back then she'd thought he'd been trying to schmooze her. She hadn't had time to appreciate what she had before she'd lost it, and this time she had no intention of making the same mistake.

After climbing in and revving the engine, he pulled out onto the quiet main street, and she settled back, trying to act nonchalant while she wanted to squirm with excitement.

'Can I ask you something?'

'Sure.'

He shot a quick glance at her, the concern in his eyes troubling. 'You had a funny look on your face for a while back there. Did that place remind you of your folks?'

She could have bluffed her way out of it, but being so close to him, the faintest waft of cedar tickling her nose and a palpable heat radiating off him, she could barely think straight let alone come up with a half-plausible excuse.

Crinkling her nose, she said, 'Yeah, it did.'

Before she could blink, he'd pulled over and

turned to her and cupped her cheek, his touch instantly soothing. 'Want to talk about it?'

'You mean my parents or their time warp coffee house?'

Her forced jocularity fell flat as he drew her closer and brushed a gentle kiss across her lips, a kiss of understanding, of support, and she slid her hands up his chest, gripping his T-shirt, feeling more anchored and safe in that moment than she ever had before.

'You said you left Rainbow Creek not long after I did. From what they told me before I left, once I was out of the picture everything would be fine with you guys. What happened?'

Sighing, she reached for the end of her ponytail and twisted it till she couldn't twist anymore.

She didn't want to dredge this up, not today, the first day of the rest of their lives, but he'd asked. Besides, she had no hope of denying him anything when he cradled her close like this, making her feel more cherished and secure than she'd ever been.

'You name it, they did it. Lying. Manipulating. Controlling.'

Swallowing down the bitterness that arose whenever she thought about their final show-down, she forced herself to continue.

'My nan died when I was sixteen. She and Mum never got on, so Nan left me everything. I never really asked how much it was all worth, but I knew it had to be hefty. Apparently, once her assets were sold, all the cash would be tied up in a trust fund I couldn't access till I was twenty-one.'

'Wow, so you're loaded. Good to know you're not just with me for my money.'

With a tender grin, he brushed a strand of hair off her face, and she leaned into his palm, relishing his support, finding the need to keep talking surprising. She hated rehashing old stuff, painful stuff, but this was strangely cathartic.

'My folks knew how much I wanted to move to Melbourne. It was all I talked about as a teenager, and I made it pretty clear that once I came into Nan's money I was out of there. Not because I didn't love them or Rainbow Creek, it was just my dream, you know?'

'I know, sweetheart.'

He did, considering the reason he'd left all

those years ago was to let her pursue it. Crazy, infuriating man.

'After you left we had this huge fight, a real monster blowout. They tried to tell me how stupid I'd been in marrying you, how I'd regret it for the rest of my life, and that it just proved I wasn't ready to take control of Nan's money.'

Realisation dawned in his eyes, and she nodded. 'Yeah, that's right. Nan's will stipulated I could have the money at eighteen, but Mum and Dad lied to me. They knew how much moving to Melbourne meant to me, but they manipulated the situation for God only knows what reason.'

Even now, she couldn't comprehend why they'd done it, apart from the fact they'd wanted to keep her chained to their sides like a little kid.

Resting his hands on her shoulders, he gave her a gentle squeeze. 'They must have loved you a lot to go to those lengths to get a few more years with you.'

'That's not love, that's being controlling!' Though a tiny seed of doubt unfurled amidst her residual bitterness as she absorbed what he'd said. What if he was right?

She'd never considered the fact they might have acted out of love, that they might have wanted more time with her before she left town.

Instead, she'd been so focused on the betrayal, of them lying to her, of how they'd blurted the truth in anger and would never have told her otherwise, that she'd shut herself off to their possible motivations.

Smoothing back her hair, he said, 'What they did was wrong, and I'm not trying to tell you what to do here, but I saw the pain on your face back there. Maybe you need to sort things out with them?'

The mere thought congealed the ice cream in her tummy, and she surreptitiously rubbed it, wishing he wasn't so damned intuitive, knowing it was part of his charm.

'Maybe.' She slid her hands up his chest to cup his face. 'In the meantime, thanks for being such an amazing, caring man.'

'I try.'

His self-deprecating shrug and exaggerated modest expression had her chuckling, and she planted a quick kiss on his lips before giving him a gentle shove towards the steering wheel.

'As a distraction technique, that was pretty lousy. Now, drive and take me to this great surprise.'

'Right. We'll be there in two minutes.'

'Any hints?'

She turned to face him, taking any opportunity to look at him. He hadn't shaved this morning—after much badgering on her part, when she'd pleaded with him to leave the sexy stubble alone—and with his dark hair ruffled by the wind, what appeared to be his oldest polo shirt, bearing a faded athletic logo, and a pair of charcoal cargo shorts, he could have been a poster boy for a weekend by the sea.

'I won't give you any hints if you keep staring at me like that.'

Her gaze lifted to his, her breath catching at the blatant desire there.

Would it always be like this between them, the instant flare of fire deep within, the breathless feeling, the drop-away tummy?

Surely something this powerful, this intense, this *physical*, should fade? But it hadn't, not in the six long years they'd been apart, and it never would if she had any say in it.

Reaching out to run a fingertip over his stubbled jaw, she murmured, 'I was just admiring this.'

'I could tell.'

His eyes darkened to molten silver an instant before he ducked across the seat and hauled her against him, crushing her breasts to his rock-hard chest, plastering his lips to hers in the type of scintillating, breath-stealing kiss only he could deliver.

Like a torch touched to tinder-dry kindling, she combusted, heat exploding in a chemical reaction which left her gasping as he broke the kiss.

The sounds of ragged breathing filled the car as she flopped back into the passenger seat and he ran a hand through his hair, his shocked expression mirroring hers.

'If you want to make it back to Melbourne and your café by nightfall, you better stop staring at me like that.'

'Melbourne? Where's that?'

Smiling, she raised a hand to her sensitised lips, touching them, savouring the residual tingle, wishing she'd had the sense to get Anna to cover for her tonight, too.

'You're a bad girl.'

He turned the ignition till the diesel engine rumbled to life and, with a pat on the dashboard, steered the lumbering ute into the deserted street.

'And you love it.'

'I do,' he said, so softly she barely caught it, and a thrill—part exultation, part fear—shot through her.

She'd realised she still loved him last night, but what about him? He'd wanted to get reacquainted, but did that mean he felt the same way?

Yes, he'd found her and, yes, he wanted to reunite, but he hadn't exactly said those magical three little words yet, no matter how much he hinted at it.

'You don't have anything to worry about.'

'Who said I'm worried?'

She shot a glance at him, and, while he hadn't taken his eyes off the road, the corners of his mouth were twitching with amusement.

'You're playing with your hair. You always do that when you're worried about something.'

Eyes narrowed, she shot him a mock-exasperated glare. 'Mind reading again?'

'Just observant.'

Tossing her ponytail over her shoulder, and clasping her hands in her lap to stop fiddling, she said, 'What would I have to be worried about, anyway?'

Apart from the fact they were moving so fast and she was willing to risk everything and take a chance on their marriage despite what had happened last time round?

'You're scared.'

He indicated and turned left, pulling onto a dirt track with fine white sand along the edges, indicating they weren't far from the beach.

'About us,' he added, as if he needed to! 'You're worried I'll let you down, maybe even leave again.'

'Is that your professional opinion?'

He darted a quick glance at her, smiling when he saw her tongue firmly planted in her cheek.

'From a construction CEO moonlighting as a shrink, yes, it is. But you've got nothing to be concerned about. I'm not going to hurt you.'

She hoped not, for it had left her heartbroken six years ago; this time it would devastate her.

Determined not to spoil the mood for his surprise, she touched his arm. 'Okay. Are we nearly there yet?'

Apparently satisfied with her change of topic, he waved his hand towards the left.

'Just around this next bend.'

'So what is this place…'

She trailed off as he negotiated the tight hairpin bend, her mouth dropping open. 'Oh, wow.'

Smiling at her shock, he slowed the ute to a crawl to give her time to appreciate the full impact of the view. 'Not bad, huh?'

'It's beautiful.'

She'd never been an ocean girl, spending all her life in dusty, dry Rainbow Creek before falling for the big-city lights of Melbourne, but with this incredible vista before her—deep indigo ocean dotted with whitecaps crashing onto pristine sand, the occasional dolphin flipping through the waves and an endless expanse of bright blue sky—she definitely understood the attraction.

Pulling over to the side of the road, he turned to face her. 'This isn't the surprise.'

Her eyebrows shot up. 'It isn't?'

'Uh-uh. That's around the next bend.'

'You're such a tease.'

She sent him a coy glance from beneath lowered lashes which said he could tease her any time, any where.

Chuckling, he indicated, did a quick check over his shoulder and pulled back onto the track, the ute doing a little sideways skid that had her laughing along with him.

'What is it with boys and their big toys?'

He shrugged, his attention fixed on negotiating another hairpin bend. 'Don't you know? We never grow up.'

That wasn't entirely true. While Blane's blundering red-and-white ute with its fancy chrome bull bar might be a big boy's toy, he'd grown up in all the ways it counted, namely into a strong, capable man not afraid to revisit the past and come clean as to why he'd done what he did.

It must have taken a lot of courage for him to walk into her café that first day, not knowing how she'd react, ready to bare his soul to her.

Then again, maybe he had known how she'd react for she'd always been his, from the first minute he'd smiled that sunny, lopsided smile at her six years earlier.

'You're plenty grown up for me,' she purred, laughing as he growled, gripping onto the dashboard and holding her breath as he rounded the bend, the anticipation buzzing through her body an absolute rush.

'What do you think?'

Swivelling her head to the left, she couldn't believe her eyes. If the ocean view on the right was something else, the enormous mansions lining the track were out of this world.

'Those are some houses,' she said, admiring the clean, crisp lines of the beautiful houses and the way they blended into the environment.

'Here's the one I really want you to see.'

He swung into a gravel drive, the ute bumping on a potholed, deeply riveted driveway which wound its way slowly upward. She craned her neck, a little confused as to why he'd drive her out here to see some house.

Snapping her fingers, she said, 'You're

building a place out here. Is that the surprise? You want to show off your work?'

'Something like that.'

He sent her an enigmatic smile, his eyes crinkling into those adorable lines she'd personally kissed each and every one, last night, as the ute crested the drive and the land plateaued to reveal a house.

Not just any house.

The most exquisite house she'd ever seen.

A house she knew intimately.

A house she'd envisioned so clearly many years before.

'I can't believe it,' she breathed out on a sigh, gobsmacked by what she was seeing, her head computing it, her heart aching with the poignancy of what this meant.

Perched on an outcrop, her dream house—the one she'd imagined them living in one day and told him about when they'd first married—saluted the cloudless sky with its sharp triangular lines, classic two-storey design and enough glass to redo the Louvre.

Pale blues, dove greys and pristine whites highlighted the light, breezy feel of it, instantly bringing to mind images of soft spring days, fluffy white clouds and a man with incredible grey eyes.

Her dream house. He'd brought her to an exact replica of the house she'd wanted for the two of them.

'You built this?'

He nodded, pride tinged with a hint of bashfulness flashing across his face. 'With a little help from the odd plumber, electrician and carpenter or two. So you like it, huh?'

'Like it? I love it!'

She opened the door and jumped down, landing with both feet squarely in a mound of muddy clay, grimacing as her new tan leather ankle boots sank into the gooey mess.

'Guess I should've warned you city shoes and country living don't mix,' he drawled, the crinkles around his eyes a dead giveaway he was fighting a grin.

Sending him a mock glare, she picked one foot up at a time, the horrible slurping sound making her see the funny side and, with much laughter, she shook each foot and set off for the house.

'Don't forget I'm a country girl at heart. You coming?' she tossed over her shoulder, a flush of pleasure spreading through her body when she caught him ogling her butt, her two-hundred-dollar boots forgotten, his grin forgiven.

'Oh, yeah.'

He fell into step beside her, taking hold of her hand and swinging it between them. 'Want to take a look inside?'

'Will the owner mind?'

They stopped at the front door, an elaborate double-door with frosted glass, so she couldn't see inside no matter how hard she tried.

'Why don't you ask him?'

Realisation dawned as he squeezed her hand, a tiny thrill of anticipation racing through her.

'This is yours?'

'Ours.'

Pulling her flush against him, he slid his arms around her waist, anchoring her nice and tight.

'I started building this the moment I located you. I wanted to prove how much you mean to me, how much I believe in our future together.'

Tears filled her eyes, brimming over and trickling down her cheeks. 'So you did remember?'

'That this is your dream house for us? Yeah, I remembered.'

He brushed her tears away with his thumbs, following their trail with his lips. 'How could I forget? How could I forget anything about you when you're the only woman in the world for me? Always have been, always will be.'

'Stop it,' she sobbed, burying her face in his chest, comforted by his cedar smell, her heart overflowing with so much love for this incredible man she thought it would burst.

Pulling away, he brushed her mouth with his in a slow, sensual kiss that reached all the way down to her very soul. 'What, stop loving you? Never.'

'I love you, too,' she said, sniffling and laughing and crying all at the same time, her last lingering doubts fading away under the intensity of his love and the lengths he'd gone to in proving it.

With the smile of a man who'd just won the lottery, he slipped an arm around her waist, drew

her close, and gestured towards the soaring
glass-enclosed atrium entrance.

'Come on. Why don't I show you around our
place?'

CHAPTER SEVEN

CAMRYN floated through the house, her feet barely touching the floor.

With Blane's arm firmly anchored around her waist, his body heat enveloping her in a warm, intimate cocoon and his low, soothing tone washing over as he spoke of his plans, *their* plans for the future, she couldn't be happier.

Until they entered the master bedroom, and her dreams of happily ever after blew away on the brisk ocean breeze entering from the open window.

'What's that little nook over there for?' She had to ask the question, needed to hear him say it, even though she already knew the answer.

The rest of the palatial home screamed family, from the huge rumpus room to the family games room, from the five spare bedrooms to the family-friendly meals area, and the little added-on space within the grand master bedroom could only be for one thing. A makeshift nursery. Large enough to fit a cradle and feeding chair and, in Blane's case, a whole lot of futile dreams.

How could she have been so stupid? She'd meant to tell him as soon as she realised she loved him but had been so wrapped up in their reconciliation, so high after realising he loved her as much as she loved him, that the truth had taken a back seat to their reunion.

They'd never discussed having kids in Rainbow Creek. Heck, they'd practically been kids themselves back then.

Ironically, it wouldn't have been an issue back then. But what she'd gone through the last few years would have an impact now, with the potential to ruin any chance of happiness before they'd really begun.

'That's a temporary baby station,' he said, sending her a bashful smile which broke her heart. 'My sisters have two kids apiece and were always going on about the risk of SIDS being reduced dramatically if you keep the baby in your room for the first six months, so I figured

NICOLA MARSH 181

it was easier to add the extra room into the plans now rather than fiddle with the house later.'

He made it sound so logical, as if planning for future babies was the most natural thing in the world. Maybe it was, but not for her. She'd given up on that dream about the same time she'd given up on ever finding him again.

'Hey, don't you like it?'

He snuggled up to her from behind, sliding his arms around her waist and holding her close, his chin resting on her head as she blinked rapidly, the sudden sting of tears burning her eyes and clogging her throat.

'It's not that,' she rasped, clearing her throat several times, knowing she had to tell him the truth, hating what this was going to do to them.

He wanted kids.

Probably a whole band of boisterous, beach-combing ruffians to fill every room of this fabulous house with love and laughter.

She could see the vision so clearly in her head, a vision she'd deliberately obliterated when she'd hobbled from the hospital that last time.

But now, in this man's arms, in her dream

house, the vision was real, very real, and she wanted it as much as he did. Sadly, wanting something so badly you could taste it and having it come true were worlds apart.

She had to tell him so.

Gently turning her in the circle of his arms, his smile faded, the tenderness in his eyes quickly replaced by concern as she slowly raised her stricken gaze to meet his.

'Hey, what's wrong? Am I moving too fast? I know we never talked about kids but I thought—'

'It's not that.'

She laid a finger against his lips, wishing she could trace its sensual contours, cover them with hers, and lose herself in the moment, effectively eliminating the need for words or painful truths.

But she had to do this. It was the only way if they were to have any chance, remote as it was.

With her heart aching from the unfairness of it all and the growing confusion on his face, she dropped her hand and eased out of his embrace.

'I don't think I can have children.'

His eyes widened in shock, the cobalt flecks sparking to life as she shook her head and crossed to an enormous window overlooking the ocean, bracing herself against the frame and staring out at the endless azure expanse.

'I've had pelvic inflammatory disease for the last few years. It's been pretty bad. The docs did exploratory surgery, cleared away scar tissue, had a general poke around. They said it's not impossible for me to have kids, but it's going to be tough. Very tough...' She trailed off, suddenly overwhelmed by the thought of not giving this incredible man the babies he deserved, and she inhaled a sharp breath, hoping the sea air would stave off the deep, heart-wrenching sob bubbling in the back of her throat.

'Sweetheart, I'm so sorry.'

He came up behind her and hugged her close, his body a solid, comforting backdrop in an unfair, unsteady world. 'Is there anything I can do?'

She shook her head, wishing he could fix this as well as he'd fixed the empty hole he'd left in her life by simply walking back into it.

'This doesn't affect us, you know. We'll face whatever happens together.'

Not affect them? That wasn't entirely true, and

they both knew it. This house clearly symbolised his hopes for the future, a future which might not include kids no matter how much she wanted it to.

Sighing, she turned to face him, propping her butt on the sill and bracing her hands on his chest.

'You wouldn't have built this house, designed it as a family home, unless you wanted to fill it with a bunch of kids, yeah?'

His face softened when she said the K word, and, while he might have said it wouldn't affect them, she had her answer before he spoke.

'Guess I'm tired of being the doting uncle to my sisters' broods. I want in on the action. The mess, the fun, the laughs, I want it all.'

A tiny crack appeared in her heart, splintering outwards at the realisation of how incredible he really was, and what she'd be giving up if she did the right thing and set him free to follow his dream with someone else.

'Listen to me, Cam. The docs said it'd be hard, so we'll try. And if it doesn't work, we'll explore other options. Nothing's impossible as long as we're together.'

Reaching out, he drew her closer, and she let

him, eager to believe his words yet knowing she'd be selfish for taking a risk on them when she might never be able to give him the family he deserved, her hands sliding up his chest, anchoring her while the rest of her world spun out of control.

'Cam, look at me.'

She shook her head, keeping her gaze firmly fixed on his chest. Looking into those incredible grey eyes right now would be tantamount to staring into an eclipse: she'd be burned eternally.

'I want you in my life, as my wife, for ever,' he murmured, his lips grazing her temple while he stroked her back in long, slow movements.

Relaxing into the protective circle of his arms, she closed her eyes, savouring the heat flowing from his strong, sure palms through her hooded top and onto her skin, relishing the tiny sparks shooting through her as he trailed butterfly kisses down her cheek before brushing her lips with his.

She moaned and tilted her face up to receive his kiss, all too aware it could be their last if she set him free, determined to make the most of it.

'Let's make this work,' he whispered against

the side of her mouth a moment before covering her mouth with his, and she stiffened as the reality of what they were doing flashed through her mind.

They could share a million bone-melting, heart-warming kisses, and it wouldn't change a thing. She might be infertile. He wanted kids. Different goals equalled separate lives.

'I can't do this.'

She broke away from him, the wrench devastating as she craved the comfort of his arms with every breath she took, knowing after what she was about to say she might never have that privilege again.

Whirling around to stare at the view again and swipe a hand across her wet cheeks, she took several deep breaths, needing to calm down before she broke down.

'I love you, Cam.'

'I know.'

Her voice wavered with sadness and unshed tears as she wished there could be a way around this.

But there wasn't. He wanted a family, she couldn't give him that, and the longer this went on, the more she fell in love with him, the harder it would be.

Tugging on the end of her plait, she swung back to face him, trying to harden her heart and failing at the sight of the hurt in his eyes.

'I love you, too, but I don't want to give you false hope. If I can't conceive naturally, it's going to be a rough road ahead. Countless tests, prodding and poking from docs, counselling, sperm donation rooms, hormone injections, implants, procedures, and that's even before going down the IVF road.'

Taking a deep breath, she blew it out long and slow, her gaze never leaving his, beseeching him to understand. 'IVF is tougher still, and if that fails, the adoption route is even worse. Years and years of filling out forms and being fobbed off and getting our hopes up only to be disappointed. Do you really want to go through all that?'

Am I really worth it?

That was the real question she was asking, her heart hoping for a miracle, her head knowing she was crazy for putting him in this position.

He ran a hand across his jaw, across the stubble

she loved so much, his expression bleak but his warm, steady gaze fixed on her.

'I'm willing to try if you are. Nothing's impossible for us. And if it's not to be, well, we'll deal with that, too.'

'No!'

The refusal exploded out of her, the pain slicing her in two. She needed to make him understand how much she loved him, how much she was willing to give up in order for him to follow his dream.

He'd once done the same for her, the least she could do was return the favour. He deserved it. He deserved his dream as much as she'd deserved hers.

Grabbing his hand, she held it between both of hers, willing him to listen.

'Don't you get it? I love you so much I want you to be happy. I want you to have the family you want. And I don't want you to go getting your hopes up when it may never happen for us.'

She broke off as he opened his mouth to reply, placing a finger to his lips to silence him.

'No, let me finish. These past few months, rediscovering each other, have been amazing, but I don't want to hold you back. If you want a family, maybe it's better we end things now.'

There, she'd said it, and her heart ached with the agony of it. Losing him now would leave a gaping, irreparable hole in her life, and she'd never recover from it. But better that than live with the guilt she'd bound him to her for her own selfish reasons and held him back from having the family he truly deserved.

Silence. Punctuated by the occasional far-off cry of a seagull, the sound of a ride-on lawnmower.

'I've already told you what I want. And that's you.'

Placing a finger under her chin and tilting it up, he said, 'I want *you*, Cam.'

He brushed a thumb across her chin repeatedly, soft, soothing, rhythmic. 'It has always been you. If kids aren't in the picture, it doesn't matter. I love you, I'll always love you, and the two of us are going to have a great life together. It was just the two of us at the start, and that's enough for me. You and me, partners, lovers, best friends, for ever.'

She'd laid it out for him so he wasn't under any illusions, and he still wanted her. Just her.

Hope swept through her, and she rode the wave, his sincere pledge dousing her doubts, silencing her voice of reason for an all-too-brief moment, filling her with the teensiest amount of optimism they could make this work.

She desperately wanted to believe him, wished she had as much faith in them as he did. But no amount of wishing and hoping could eradicate the simple truth. He wanted kids, she couldn't have them. And while he was adamant she'd be enough for him now, what if his love for her dwindled and turned to despair when she couldn't give him the one thing he needed the most?

He'd left her once before, what would stop him doing it again? She'd recovered from the heartache last time through sheer hard work, determined to obliterate her pain and fill the void he'd left with business. But if it happened again, after she'd fallen so irrefutably, cataclysmically in love with him all over again, she'd never recover.

Drawing a shaky breath, she laid her hand against his cheek, drawing on every ounce of inner strength she possessed. She needed to make him understand. Yet his tender expression stole her breath and increased her torment tenfold.

'You're the most extraordinary, wonderful, special guy, and I love you with all my heart. But I can't do this.'

'Yeah, you can.'

Pulling her close, he leaned his forehead against hers, their noses touching, the pure male scent of him filling her senses. 'We're in this for the long haul, and we'll deal with it all. Just go with the flow.'

As if to prove his point, he slanted a slow, searing kiss across her lips, setting her pulse racing and her insides trembling.

'But—'

'Go with the flow,' he repeated, smiling against her mouth as he moved a tad to the left, his pelvis snuggling into hers, showing her exactly how ready he was to go with the flow.

A shudder of longing shot through her, urging her to believe in the man she loved, to ignore her doubts.

He pulled away and stared down at her, his

grey eyes magnetic. 'You're it for me, Cam. For always.' His lips slowly descended to meet hers in a soul-reaching, shivery kiss before he whispered against her mouth, 'Let me love you.'

Her resolve melted away on a river of hot, intense desire, her need to have him obliterating her anguish at never being enough for him, swift and powerful and all-consuming.

Her heart quivered, her legs wobbled, and her hands shook as she placed them against his chest, so warm, so solid, and slowly nodded. 'But there's no furniture.'

'Who needs furniture?'

His smile, as intimate as the heavenly kiss they'd just shared, set her pulse racing as he tugged on her hand and pointed to a pile of neatly folded drop sheets in the corner of the room. 'Looks like the painters haven't used those yet.'

Chuckling, she sent him a teasing look from beneath lowered lashes. 'My, my, very inventive.'

With a low groan, he pulled her flush against him. 'You drive me wild.'

This was it. Her last chance to drive home the

ramifications of their reunion despite the obstacles facing them.

But with the man of her dreams holding her, caressing her, promising to love her unconditionally, she threw her reservations out the window and let them float away on the brisk ocean breeze.

She had a lifetime to live with the agony of not being able to add to their family. Right now, she needed to lose herself in him.

Her soul aching with the depth of her love for this amazing man, she raised her gaze to his. 'Show me.'

'It'll be my pleasure.'

Releasing her hand, he unbuttoned her top, slipping buttons through loops with slow precision, her breath catching each and every time his fingers grazed her skin.

Empowered by the adoration in his eyes, she shimmied out of it, her pulse skittering and jumping like a wild thing when he reached out and trailed a finger ever so slowly from one collarbone to the next, dipping briefly into her cleavage, teasing her, building the anticipation till she could barely stand.

'Now, let me show you exactly how wild you drive me.'

A brief shiver rippled through her as his lips brushed against hers, once, twice, before he moved across the room, shook out several drop cloths and placed them on the ground as if laying out an ermine blanket for a princess to picnic on.

'Care to join me?'

His slow, sexy smile captivated her, and she moved towards him, impelled by an over-whelming need to make memorable love with her husband.

The air around them seemed electrified as she put one foot in front of the other, drifting towards him, his gaze as soft as a caress, travelling over her face, her body, his adoring expression sending her spirits soaring and making her body tremble.

Taking his outstretched hand, she let out a ragged breath as they sank onto the floor together, and in a flurry of discarded clothes and desperate fondling and frantic caresses, with the late afternoon sun streaming through the windows and casting sensuous shadows against the stark walls, Camryn ignored her reservations, her worries and the conviction she would never be enough for him, and lost herself in the pleasure of her incredibly special husband.

CHAPTER EIGHT

BLANE followed the exuberant squeals coming from the backyard of his youngest sister's place, preparing for the launch of two tiny bodies into his arms.

As much as he loved Jodi, he knew he wouldn't spend half as much time here if it wasn't for the twins, James and Jemma.

Patting down his pockets to make sure he hadn't forgotten this week's treat, he rounded the corner and pushed through the back gate, bracing himself as the twins lifted their heads in unison at the squeak of the rusty hinge, caught sight of him, and rocketed out of the sandpit, making a beeline straight for him.

'Hey, kiddos.'

He bent down and opened his arms a split second before two sturdy bodies hurled themselves at him, wrapping grubby hands around his neck and slobbering sloppy kisses on his cheeks.

'Uncle Blay, Uncle Blay!' they yelled in chorus, trying to outdo each other in the clambering stakes, grabbing his hair, his ears, and giggling like they'd sculled a litre of fizzy drinks.

'Hey, you two.' He tickled and hugged them till the noise level reached ear-splitting levels, disentangling arms and legs before setting James on his feet and Jemma alongside him. 'Have you been good for your mum this week?'

'Uh-huh.' James, bold as brass, blue eyes wide and expectant, stared at his pockets while his sister, suddenly shy, stuck her thumb in her mouth.

'I'm the one you should be asking.'

He smiled as Jodi waddled towards them, trying to balance a tray laden with fruit, water and dry crackers, her round belly protruding much further than last week. 'Ask me again why I wanted another one after the terrible two.'

Taking the tray from her, he dropped a kiss on her cheek. 'Terrific two, you mean.'

As she eased into a chair, her face creased into a fond smile as she saw the twins standing still like a couple of expectant angels, not making a sound.

'They are pretty terrific most of the time. Though you know they're only ever quiet like this when you bribe them as you do every week.'

Pouring a glass of iced water and handing it to her, he said, 'It's not bribery, it's spoiling my favourite niece and nephew.'

'Don't let Sandy and Monica hear that. You know they think their kids are godsends.'

Laughing, he bent down to the twins' level and pretended to rummage in his pockets.

'Hmm…what have I got here?'

At the familiar question, the twins abandoned their good behaviour and started climbing all over him again.

'James! Jemma!'

He winked at Jodi over James's shoulder, disengaging two pairs of cloying hands before producing matching miniature diggers from each pocket.

'Wow,' the twins said in unison, eyes wide as they grabbed the brightly coloured toy earth movers, already running for the sandpit to bury their latest treasure.

'Hey, what do you say? And what about your snack?'

The twins pulled up short at the sound of their mother's firm tone and turned back to him. 'Thaaank yooou, Uncle Blaaaay…'

They drew out each word in the usual way kids did when told to thank someone, whirling away the minute he smiled at them.

'They can have their snack later,' he said, catching sight of Jodi's frown. 'Let them have a play.'

Rolling her eyes, she offered him the fruit platter. 'You're a pushover. Wait till you have kids of your own. You'll see.'

His smile faded as he selected a bunch of grapes and slid onto the wooden bench opposite.

'Hey, what did I say?'

'Nothing.'

He popped several grapes into his mouth at once, chewing thoughtfully, wondering how much he should tell his sister.

'Come on, bro. Spill it. This has to be about a woman.'

Not just *a* woman. *The* woman.

The woman he'd half fallen in love with the moment he'd first laid eyes on her, the woman he'd walked away from six years earlier, the woman to complete him, to make his dreams come true.

But she still harboured doubts. He'd seen it in her expressive eyes when she'd told him about her difficulty bearing kids, he'd seen it in her tense body language on the trip back to Melbourne afterwards.

He should be ecstatic she loved the house and had agreed to give their marriage a second chance, but he couldn't dispel the gloomy feeling that something wasn't quite right, that Cam didn't believe him when he'd said she was all he needed to make his life complete.

Eyes narrowed, Jodi stabbed an apple slice in his direction.

'She doesn't want kids! That's why you got that funny look on your face when I mentioned kids of your own.'

Shaking his head, he gulped down a glass of water to ease the sudden constriction in his throat at the thought of never having children.

'It's not as simple as that.'

'Then how simple is it?'

Knowing she'd never let him leave without some snippet of the truth, he sat back and interlocked his hands behind his head.

'It's Cam.'

Jodi sat bolt upright, wincing as her belly grazed the table. '*The* Cam? As in the teenager-you-married-then-walked-away-from Cam? As in love-of-your-life Cam? The Cam we've all heard about but never met?'

He smiled, used to his sister's dramatics. 'That's the one.'

'What's going on with you two? Did you find her? Are you reuniting?'

Jodi rested her folded arms on the top of her belly and glared at him. 'Come on, bro, spill it before I go into premature labour trying to get the teensiest bit of gossip out of you.'

Chuckling, he tilted his face up to the sun, closed his eyes and enjoyed the warmth on his face, knowing it would drive his nosy sister batty.

'Blane, I'm not kidding. Either you tell me this very minute or I'll get Sandy and Mon and Mum on the phone in a conference call right this very minute and—'

'Okay, okay, hang on to your baby bonnet.'

He opened an eye and squinted at her. 'Actually, that conference call mightn't be a bad idea. Save you the trouble of getting onto the phone and spreading the news the minute I walk out of here.'

'Funny guy.' She waggled her finger at him in the same way he'd seen her admonish the twins countless times before. 'Weeell? What's going on with you two? And, more importantly, when do we get to meet her?'

Opening his eyes, he sat up and reached for an apricot, cramming it into his mouth and chewing quickly, aware his sis wouldn't hold out much longer. Curious cats had nothing on her.

Taking a slug of water, he leaned across the table and sent her a conspiratorial wink. 'What's going on? We're back together, that's what.'

Jodi squealed and clapped her hands. 'I knew it! That's brilliant, I'm so happy for you.'

'I'm happy, too,' he said and meant it.

When he'd first located Cam and put his plans for the house into action, he'd hoped the powerful connection they'd once had would still be alive, that she'd be willing to hear him out and take another chance on them. Now they were a couple again, he could hardly believe his luck.

'I've never seen you like this,' Jodi said, her curiosity evident in her lowered voice, for his youngest sister never spoke in anything lower than a bellow. 'I'm really looking forward to meeting the woman who can make you look like that!'

'You'll meet her soon enough.'

When he'd had enough time to warn her about the Andrews clan and the overwhelming barrage of noise, warmth and bear hugs she'd be at the receiving end of.

Jodi tilted her chin up in the classic challenging pose of all the Andrews sisters. 'When?'

Smiling, he pushed the fruit platter across to her. 'Here, junior needs his or her daily dose of vitamins.'

'Don't try to distract me, it won't work.' She popped a plump raspberry into her mouth, wincing slightly at its tartness. 'I want to meet your wife.'

'You will.'

He just wanted her to himself for a bit longer.

After six years apart, six years too long, was that too much for a guy to ask?

'So why the funny look when I mentioned you two having kids?'

He should have known. Jodi would never let up, but he'd be damned if he sat here and discussed Cam's medical history with his nosy sister.

'Just leave it alone, Jode. We've only just reunited, so give us a break, okay?'

She fixed him with a shrewd stare, her mouth opening in readiness to pump him for more information and he held up a hand.

'Not another word. Change the subject or I'll make sure you don't meet Cam for the next year.'

'You're no fun,' she huffed, sending him a killer glare as she nibbled a dry biscuit. 'You can't blame me for being curious.'

'Patience, Sis, patience. You'll meet her soon enough.'

As for divulging the rest, there was no way he'd be sharing their personal business with his family. The Andrews family was just that: one big happy family with kids taking a starring role.

If Cam already had doubts about his devotion

to her without the bonus of children, he didn't need his rowdy family poking their prying noses in where they didn't belong and adding to her skittishness.

Jodi frowned. 'Okay, but you better make it soon. Otherwise I'll definitely get Sandy, Mon and Mum onto you. And you won't stand a chance of holding us all at bay.'

'Too right.'

He chuckled, pushing the fruit platter closer to her as he stood. 'Now, eat up while I go and spend some time with those gorgeous kids of yours.'

As he headed for the sandpit, he couldn't help but wonder if he'd ever have any kids of his own…and coming to the same conclusion he had when Cam had first told him. If he had her in his life, it wouldn't matter. Nothing would, as long as they faced it together.

'You shaved,' Camryn accused, running a finger-tip along Blane's smooth jaw. 'And you're wearing designer jeans and a snazzy shirt! Why didn't you tell me to dress up?'

As if she wasn't in enough of a tizz meeting

his family. Now she'd be inappropriately dressed, too.

He laughed and ran a hand over her hip, gliding over the summer cotton dress she'd finally flung on after pulling out half her wardrobe, his sensual touch going a long way towards calming some of her nerves.

'You look gorgeous. And it's not dressy. I just thought you might like to see me in something other than work jeans and T-shirts.'

'Actually, I like seeing you without any clothes,' she purred, sliding a hand up his chest and leaning into him, inhaling as she did so, re-assured by his familiar crisp cedar scent.

He laughed and pulled her in for a swift kiss. 'Hmm…I'm sure that would go down a treat with my family.'

His family… She'd been steeling herself all week, ever since she'd agreed to accompany him to this barbecue.

He'd made it sound casual at the time, just a small get-together, and, while she was curious after hearing so much about the Andrews family, she couldn't help but worry.

What if they didn't like her? It wasn't as if she'd had much practice playing happy families lately.

Drawing back, he rubbed her arms up and down. 'Hey, it's not going to be so bad, you'll see.'

'How much have you told them about me?'

'Enough.'

He winked and, grabbing her hand, tugged her gently towards the ute. 'Come on, they'll love you.'

That was what she was afraid of. He loved his family, had always been close to them, so she was betting his family knew about his dreams for kids, too. So where did that leave her?

She'd been honest with him on that score, and, while he'd said all the right things after their candid chat at his house, she'd caught him staring at families with kids on the odd occasion, a wistful expression on his ruggedly handsome face. That look had terrified her, as it had confirmed what she'd suspected for a while now. She would never be enough for him no matter how many times he said otherwise.

Not that she thought for one second he didn't mean it, for Blane was nothing but sincere. But what if he grew to resent her? What if the endless dramas they went through to have kids—and still failed—put a strain on their marriage they could never recover from? Or the absolute kicker: what if he left her again if she couldn't give him the family he wanted?

'They'll love you if you lose that mournful expression, that is.'

Tweaking her nose, he brushed a tender kiss across her lips, and she smiled up at him, slinging her favourite plum carryall over her shoulder. 'I'm ready.'

'That's my girl.'

Handing her up into the ute, he deliberately grazed her bare calf as he withdrew, the simple touch combining with his smouldering stare to set her heart thumping. As if it wasn't jumping around enough.

Loving how quickly and thoroughly he could turn her on with a look and the barest of touches, she sent him a seductive peep from beneath lowered lashes.

'We don't have to stay too long, do we?'

She toyed with the hem of her dress, plucking

at the scalloped edge, smoothing it where it ended on her knees, enjoying his slightly glazed expression as he gripped the steering wheel and started the engine.

'If you keep looking at me like that we won't even make it there.'

'Okay, I'll behave.'

She laid a hand on his thigh and gave it a gentle squeeze, enjoying the flexing of hard muscle beneath her palm, all too aware of exactly how that muscle felt without the denim covering. 'For now.'

Chuckling, he pulled out into the heavy city traffic, his concentration focused on navigating the traffic-logged roads around the Docklands while she tried to keep her mind off the constant nagging worry that the kids issue was bigger than he was willing to acknowledge.

Camryn's face ached.

Her cheeks were stiff and her mouth hurt from too much smiling. Blane's family were amazing. They'd welcomed her, chatted with her, plied her with food, showered her with attention, and she'd smiled through it all until her gut had seized and her heart bled as they'd fielded the inevitable ribbing question for a married couple: 'so when are you two lovebirds having kids?'

Blane had deflected that one nicely, but she'd caught the significant look passing between his folks, as if judging her for possibly not wanting kids.

Well, she'd have to get used to it. Either that or tell a bunch of people she'd only just met her personal problems, and she had no intention of doing that yet.

She might have laughed at the incessant teasing from his sisters and relaxed in the sprawling homestead on a half-acre block in outer suburbia, but they still weren't her family.

Her family... It was times like this she missed her folks, her mum in particular. They'd always been close, she'd always confided in her, and during her harrowing health ordeal she'd wished for her mum's comforting hugs too many times to remember.

Ever since Blane had sowed the seed that maybe, just maybe, her folks had done what they'd done out of love rather than an awful desire to control her, she'd been wondering if it was time to lay the past to rest, to head home and give her folks a chance to explain.

It wasn't as if they hadn't tried to breach the gap, but she'd slammed the door in their faces, metaphorically, every single time. Until they'd stopped trying.

Coming here, surrounded by genuine warmth and happiness and familial love, rammed home how much she missed her own family. Being welcomed by the Andrews family as Blane's wife was lovely. Maybe it was time to reintroduce her family to her husband.

'Hiding away won't work. They'll hunt you down eventually.'

Blane slid his arms around her waist from behind, enveloping her in welcome warmth, cuddling her close. 'They love you, you know.'

Turning in the circle of his arms, she slung her arms around his neck. 'Your family's great.'

Some of the tension around his jaw eased as he snuggled her closer. 'Can I let you in on a little secret?'

'Shoot.'

'I was worried about you being thrown in the deep end meeting the whole clan at once.'

He paused, his arms tightening as if he expected her to bolt. 'Facing Sandy, Monica and Jodi in all their nosy glory. You've been a real trouper.'

Her heart clenched. He looked so happy she'd passed the family test with flying colours, when in fact the last few hours had served to deepen the chasm between them.

She'd never felt so torn, wanting him so badly it hurt, knowing she couldn't give him what he wanted.

And, as painful as it was, seeing him with his nieces and nephews today showed her that no matter what he said, having only her would eventually, one day, not be enough.

Pain sliced through her, swift and deep, cutting her determination, weakening her resolve, at the thought of letting him go. But there was no other way. How could she not? She loved him that much. He'd once let her go to follow her dream, she'd have to do the same for him no matter how much it would tear her apart.

'Oh-oh, you've got that face again.'

She managed a small smile while her insides churned with dread at the enormity of what she had to do.

'What face?'

'This one.'

He pulled a tight-lipped, frowning, cross-eyed face, drawing a chuckle from her.

'I call it your "thinking too much" face.'

He smoothed a finger between her brows, his touch soothing, as she wished he could erase the ache in her heart as easily as the lines from her forehead. 'It always worries me. It means you're deliberating something big or going to deliver news I won't like. Correct?'

He knew her too well. However, now wasn't the time or place to get into what she was thinking.

'I'm just tired. The café was jam-packed last night, and I had to do some inventory ordering after we closed.'

'And you're exhausted after letting the twins clamber all over you. I know the feeling.'

He leaned closer and brushed a kiss across her lips, a soft, lingering kiss that touched her soul. 'You really were amazing today. Thank you.'

'For what?'

Drawing back, he scanned her face as if searching for an answer she couldn't give him.

'For making an effort, for being here, but most of all for being you.'

Her breath caught at the adoration in his gaze, and, at that moment, with the squeals of excited children, the low rumble of desultory conversation on a warm Sunday afternoon, and the distant cackle of a kookaburra in the background, she knew. Setting him free would be the hardest thing she'd ever have to do.

She loved this man, heart and soul, always had, always would. Staring into his handsome face with its bronzed skin, crinkly lines around the eyes and perpetual smile, she knew he was her future, her destiny. And she had to walk away from him...

Trying to ignore the dull ache spreading through her chest, squeezing her heart till she thought it would burst, robbing her lungs of air and the ability to speak, she closed her eyes, unable to bear looking into his beautiful eyes one second longer.

'Hey, that was a compliment,' he said, brushing

her hair off her face, the slight rasp of his calloused fingers sending a shiver down her spine.

'I know.'

.She had no option but to open her eyes, to let him glimpse the devastation ripping her apart.

'You're crying! Are you okay? Hell, I knew I should've eased you into meeting them one family at a time rather than something this big.'

She shook her head, blinking rapidly, and laid a stilling hand on his arm as he pulled away.

'No, your family is great. It's just the exhaustion catching up with me.'

Lame, lame, lame, but what could she say? *I love you more than life itself, but I have to let you go?*

Concern slashed a vertical indentation between his brows. 'You know, I'm not buying that. But I'm not going to push it, not here.'

Grabbing her hand, he pointed to the front of the house. 'Let's get out of here.'

'But what about saying goodbye?'

'Think you're up to it?'

He brushed away her tears with his thumb, the depth of his caring doing little to stem the flood she was barely managing to hold back.

'Give me a few minutes inside, then I'll pop out, thank your family, and then we can leave.'

'You sure?'

She wasn't sure about anything: about the sanity of what she was contemplating, about how she could walk away from him and, most of all, how long it would take her to pick up the pieces of her life without him in it.

'Uh-huh. Give me five minutes, and I'll be back to say goodbye.'

'Okay.'

He dropped his arms, and she instantly had the urge to burrow back into them, craving the warmth and security of his embrace.

Taking a deep breath, she lifted her head and squared her shoulders. It wouldn't do her any good to think like that anymore. Blane wouldn't be around much longer, and the thought fragmented her heart into painful little pieces all over again.

'Cam?'

'Yeah?'

'I love you so much,' he said, his tender smile radiating a depth of emotion she'd waited a lifetime for.

His declaration should have made her feel the luckiest woman in the world. Instead, with a sinking heart, she sent him a weak smile and headed for the house to marshal her defences.

For what she had to face when she set him free, she was going to need them.

CHAPTER NINE

BLANE leaned against the bar, content to nurse his beer and watch Cam strut her stuff.

She bounced around the café, flitting from one group to another, equally at ease mingling with the highfaluting advertising execs as she was with the wannabe starlets preening in the hope of being seen at Melbourne's newest hot spot.

Dressed in a slinky black wrap-around dress which highlighted her figure, her hair straight and sleek around her shoulders, and a permanent mega-watt smile on her face, she looked a million bucks.

A woman in control, in charge, and at total odds with the vulnerable mess she'd been at the barbecue.

They hadn't spoken about it since. He hadn't wanted to push his luck on the way home, not when most of the afternoon had gone so well.

Even now, a week later, he couldn't figure out what had gone wrong towards the end. He'd replayed their conversation in his head a hundred times and was still none the wiser.

As if thinking about her tugged on an invisible link binding them, she glanced up at that precise moment, sending him a dazzling smile while tucking a strand of luscious chocolate hair behind her ear with one hand, wiggling her fingers at him in a saucy wave with the other.

He raised his glass in her direction in a silent toast, chuckling as she held up a finger in a 'be with you in a sec' motion to Anna, who was frantically tugging on her arm and motioning to the kitchen, while her eyes never left his, sparkling and sassy even at a distance, her lips curving into the teasing smile he knew so well.

With a slow, deliberate wink, she turned her back on him and tilted her head towards Anna, casting a regretful look over her shoulder before following her employee into the kitchen.

He glanced at his watch, wondering if the crowd would leave soon. Launch parties for up-and-coming advertising firms weren't his thing.

He'd been to a few similar shindigs when trying to choose the right firm to represent BA Constructions, and they were all the same: guys with money to burn, girls there to be seen, loads of fake conversation and schmoozing, business and pleasure deals sealed over one too many G and Ts—though in this case, espressos all round.

This scene left him cold, and he couldn't wait to get Cam all to himself. Greedy? Hell, yeah. He'd only come because she'd said the party wouldn't last long, and every minute she spent flitting around the room playing the social butterfly was a minute too long in his books.

'Having fun?'

She'd crept up behind him, sliding her arms around his waist, pressing her breasts against his back as his mind instantly blanked and his heart beat like a drum.

'I am now.'

He turned around, regretting his action when she dropped her arms and waved at an exec strutting out the door with a blonde on each arm.

'Sorry, it's been a bit frantic tonight. Great party, huh?'

He'd never seen her so animated: her eyes sparkling, her cheeks flushed, and her mouth in a perpetual dazzling smile. She thrived on this scene; that much was obvious.

Leaning down, he slid an arm around her waist and murmured in her ear, 'Actually, it's a bit crowded for my taste. You know, I'd prefer a private party for two.'

She laughed, a fake, brittle tinkle that sent an arrow of foreboding through him.

'I like crowds. It's one of the reasons I moved to Melbourne in the first place.'

Doing a little spin on her stilettos, she tossed her hair over her shoulder and held her arms out wide. 'Guess you can't keep a good city girl down, huh?'

'I guess not.'

What had got into her? She was behaving as if she'd been serving alcohol rather than speciality coffees all night.

'So, you want to party on after this? Some of the guys mentioned hitting a club or two. I love dancing.'

She gave another bizarre twirl, though thankfully his ringing mobile saved him from answering.

Camryn watched Blane's face blanch as he clutched his mobile to his ear, a finger pressed in the other so he could hear above the din.

She didn't blame him. The noise levels in here were giving her a headache, too. She'd had some stupid, half-baked plan to show him her party side tonight, exaggerate it just a tad, accentuate their differences, maybe annoy him in the process so when she told him the truth later, it wouldn't be so difficult for him to accept they weren't so well suited after all.

Sounded simple enough, but it was just plain dumb. She didn't want Blane to hate her, and she sure didn't want to lie to him. She owed him the truth. Hopefully it would set him free.

'Stay calm. I'll be right there.' He snapped the phone shut and thrust it into his pocket, slamming his glass onto the bar before turning to her with wide eyes.

Their bleak expression shocked her. She'd never seen him anything other than upbeat, relaxed or passionate.

'What's wrong?'

'Jemma's in the hospital. The entire family's there. I have to go.'

She knew what was coming next even before he opened his mouth. Not that he had to ask. Her first instinct was to drop everything and go with him to see if the darling little girl who'd captured a small piece of her child-immune heart was okay.

'Come with me.' He grabbed her hand, his eyes beseeching, his tone desperate.

'You don't have to ask.' She stood on tiptoe and planted a quick kiss on his lips. 'Let's go.'

'What about all this?'

Touched by his concern for her when she knew how frantic he must be, she laid a silencing finger against his lips. 'It's not important. I'll have a quick word with Anna and meet you at the car, okay?'

'You're incredible.' He cupped her cheek for a moment, his love for her enveloping her in a warm, welcome shroud she hated to shrug off. 'Thank you.'

'Go.' With a gentle shove, she pushed him away, waiting till he headed for the door before letting her face crumple.

She had to find Anna, get her to wrap things up here so she could be there for Blane. He needed her. With what she'd had planned for later, it would be for the last time.

Blane swiped a hand across his eyes, but nothing could banish the gritty dryness from lack of sleep.

Not that he was the only one. Glancing around the hospital waiting room, he saw every member of his family in various sleepless poses: his folks sitting upright and rigid in the horrible orange plastic chairs, gripping each other's hands, Sandy and Monica with their heads resting on the wall at their backs, and Jodi, her forearms resting on her belly, her hands clenched.

The girls' spouses were at home looking after the kids, and he suddenly wished he could be there, away from the harsh sterility of this place with its pungent antiseptic odours, its bustling medical personnel, and the glare of fluorescent lighting on the exhausted and worried expressions etched across the faces of his family.

He hated seeing them like this, hated the thought of his precious little niece under the knife of some surgeon they'd never heard of. There'd been no choice: remove her appendix before it ruptured and possibly killed her, and, while it was a simple enough operation, he couldn't imagine a two-year-old having to go through it.

Sliding across an empty chair, he reached out and draped a comforting arm across Jodi's shoulders.

'She's going to be fine, Sis.'

Jodi lifted her head, raising red-rimmed eyes to meet his.

'Is she?' she whispered, her hands shaking so hard she had to clasp them together and rest them on her belly.

'Of course she is. Now, you need to look after this little one and let the docs do their job and look after Jem.'

He briefly laid a hand on her bulging belly, silently praying he was right. Contemplating any outcome other than a positive one was inconceivable, and, while his gut churned with worry, he could only imagine what Jodi must be going through right now.

'I just feel so helpless,' Jodi said, resting her

head against his shoulder, and he cuddled her close, wondering if wanting this parent gig so desperately was a wise choice after all.

'Mrs. Lee?'

Jodi sat bolt upright as a youngish doctor in scrubs appeared before them.

'How's Jemma? Is she all right?' she blurted, clutching his hand in a bone-cracking grip.

Blane held his breath, his gaze fixed on the doctor's mouth, willing him to speak, willing him to deliver the good news his family so desperately needed to hear.

After what seemed like an eternity, the doctor's face creased into a smile. 'Jemma's going to be fine. The surgery went well. She's in recovery now but should be out shortly, and then you can see her.'

'Thank God.'

Jodi sank against him like a lifeless doll—a heavily pregnant doll—as he sent a silent prayer of thanks heavenward.

The doctor's weary smile said he'd been through this scenario a hundred times before, and he sent them a polite nod before hurrying away as his pager beeped.

The family crowded around Jodi, and he backed off, giving them space, just as Cam appeared around the corner, tottering on high heels and trying to balance a cardboard tray bearing enough coffees to keep the entire Andrews clan up all night.

Her worried gaze noted the doctor's retreating back, skimmed over his family gathered around Jodi, before slamming into his, and what he glimpsed there took his breath away. She cared, not just the obligation type of caring for people she had just met, she really, truly cared about Jemma and for what they were all going through.

Sending her a reassuring smile, he met her halfway across the waiting room, taking the tray out of her hands, sliding it onto a nearby table and enveloping her in his arms.

'Is there news?'

'She's going to be okay,' he murmured, stroking her hair, loving how her body fit against his as if they'd been made for each other.

Which they had. He'd known it from the first moment they'd met, and how close they'd grown lately merely reinforced what he'd always known.

'Thank God.'

She sagged with relief, her hand insinuating its way between their bodies to surreptitiously swipe at her eyes.

'Hey, the worst part's over,' he said, pulling back slightly to run a thumb across her cheek, catching a lone tear as it trickled down.

'I know.'

Though from the scared gleam in her eyes, he knew she didn't believe him. Either that or something else had put that anxious look in her eyes, and he had no idea what.

'Come on, let's get out of here. You must be exhausted.'

She didn't protest, and as he slung an arm around her shoulders and headed for his family to say goodbye, he couldn't help but ponder what was going through his wife's head.

CHAPTER TEN

CAMRYN picked up the phone for the fifth time that morning before slamming the handset back in its receiver.

She had to call Blane. She'd prevaricated long enough, and last night's drama in the ER with Jemma only served to strengthen her resolve.

He loved his niece, desperately, wholeheartedly, unreservedly, and if he had that much love to give a niece, imagine how great he'd be as a father.

Setting him free was the right thing to do. Her head knew it, her heart would never catch up.

She hadn't slept a wink in the wee small hours when she'd made it back here for her first night in her brand-spanking-new apartment, hadn't been able to force a morsel of food past her lips this morning, and could barely drag her feet around the place to do a much-needed clean.

She'd never felt so drained, so lifeless, and every one of her bones ached as if she had some terrible flu.

She was sick all right: heartsick over losing the love of her life all over again.

While her heart ached and her soul emptied of joy, she picked up the phone and dialled his number, sinking into her favourite zebra-print leather chair and curling her legs up under her.

'Hello?'

He answered on the fourth ring, and her belly somersaulted at the familiar rich timbre of his voice.

'Blane, it's me. How's Jemma?'

'She's fine. Jodi just called, said she'll make a full recovery.'

'That's great,' she breathed, surprised at the depth of her relief. The little girl had wound her way into her affection, but she hadn't realised just how deeply. 'Jodi must be relieved.'

'We all are. How are you doing? You looked pretty exhausted by the time I dropped you off.'

'I am.'

She didn't elaborate, all too aware what she

had to say had to be done in person, and hoping he'd go for her plan. 'I've been doing some thinking and was wondering if you'd like to take a trip with me to Rainbow Creek.'

'Sure. When?'

He didn't miss a beat, even though he had to be more than a little surprised.

'How about this weekend? I'm tied up here every night till then.'

'Sounds great.'

He paused, as if searching for the right words, and she knew what was coming next before he spoke. 'Are you planning on seeing your parents?'

'Uh-huh.'

Among other things, namely taking him back to the place it all began for them, hoping he'd understand when she told him why she had to let him go.

'I'm so proud of you.'

He wouldn't be, not when she revealed her real motivation for heading back.

'Thanks. Look, I've got an incoming call on my mobile from a supplier, and it's important. I have to go.'

Clutching the phone, she willed him to say something else, anything else, for the simple pleasure of hearing his voice, for there wouldn't be many more times she would.

'No worries. I'll chat to you later.'

'Bye.'

She ended the call before she blurted the truth or changed her mind, staring at the phone, the dial tone humming its lifeless tune.

Flinging it onto the side table next to her, she hugged her knees tightly to her chest and rested her chin on them in the vain attempt to squeeze some of the pain out of her.

It didn't work, and, staring around the new open-plan room—her renovations completed on time thanks to Blane—with its sleek modern glass tables, funky zebra-print suite and slashes of bright-coloured artwork, she wondered if she'd ever be able to get past this.

This was the life she'd chosen: this ultra-modern apartment in the heart of the city, just across from a hip, trendy café she owned, with the freedom to do whatever she wanted whenever she wanted.

She was living the dream.

But she'd give it all away in a heartbeat if she could have kids with Blane.

Deep, painful sobs bubbled up from within, and as she squeezed her eyes shut, tears trickled down her cheeks, and she let them fall, the first time she'd cried so hard in years.

She'd been a city girl for so long now—fiercely independent, headstrong, and able to handle anything with a flick of her designer handbag and a sidestep in sky-high stilettos. She'd been that self-sufficient city girl for six years, so why the horrible, helpless feeling she couldn't get past this? Or the insane instinct to run home into her mother's comforting arms?

She had to get through this. She had to let him go to follow his dream just as he'd done for her all those years ago. She had to strengthen her resolve, get over this vulnerability, get away from reminders of him around every corner, get away from everything for a while…

Her eyes snapped open, and she dashed a hand across her cheeks. That was it. The answer to her problems. But before she could escape, she needed to take a trip of another sort.

A trip back in time.

Ochre-coloured dust rose in a billowing plume as Blane's ute pulled away, leaving Camryn no option but to sling her bag over her shoulder and head for the coffee house. She hadn't told her folks she was coming home, had counted on the element of surprise to get them past the awful awkwardness of a reunion.

Six years. She hadn't spoken to them or set foot in Rainbow Creek in six long years, and, trudging up the main street, she saw that nothing had changed.

One general store, one country pub, a grocer and a tiny church, with Ma and Pa's Coffee House tacked on the end.

Inwardly cringing at the name as she always did, she forced her feet to move down the deserted street. She'd deliberately chosen this time to arrive, knowing the town virtually shut down after dark on a Sunday, effectively shielding her from prying eyes and wagging tongues.

If she were lucky, she could say what she had to say, confront her demons, and be back in Blane's arms at the motel in under an hour.

He'd understood her need to do this on her own. No surprise considering he seemed to understand everything about her. Until she took him down to the river tomorrow and told him why she was really here; she had a feeling he wouldn't understand that at all.

As she neared the end of the street and caught her first glimpse of the tiny red brick cottage at the rear of the coffee house, a powerful wave of nostalgia crashed over her, almost knocking her off her feet.

A lamp glowed from behind closed floral curtains in the front room, and she'd bet it was the same awful elephant lamp her mum had picked up for a song at a car boot sale all those years ago. Smoke billowed from the crooked chimney, and she wrapped her arms around her middle, suddenly aware of the colder, crisper country air and her totally unsuitable chiffon top, the height of fashion in Melbourne, the height of stupidity here.

A shadow passed across the lit window, and she gasped, the enormity of what she was about to do hitting home. The prodigal daughter returns… but would she be welcome? Would she learn the truth behind her parents' selfish actions?

Taking a deep breath, she ploughed forward, long, strong strides which ate up the distance between her and the cottage. She'd had the courage to leave this house, this town, in the first place, had opened her own café in a city filled with high-quality competition, had thrived on every challenge thrown her way. Surely she could do this?

Knocking a tad loudly at the front door, she waited, clutching her bag tightly, bracing herself for the inevitable confrontation and all it would entail: the recriminations, the accusations, the judgements.

However, as the door creaked open, and she looked into her mother's open-mouthed, astonished face, all she could think about was breaching the short distance between them and flinging herself into her mum's arms.

'Cammie!'

She didn't have to make a move as her mum catapulted her short, rotund body across the threshold and flung her arms around her in a vice-like hug, crushing the air out of her, bringing tears to her eyes with the joy in her greeting.

'Hi, Mum. Long time no see, huh?'

Blinking back tears, she waited till her mum released her, preparing for the censure which would surely follow a purely instinctive greeting.

However, as she scanned her mum's lined face, the faded blue eyes, the quivering mouth, all she saw was undisguised happiness, and her heart turned over with regret.

Regret for leaving this reunion so long, regret for being so stubborn, but, most of all, regret for the years they'd lost.

'Come in, love. Your dad's out, but he'll be back soon. The kettle's on.'

And just like that she stepped back in time, taking the first tentative step to mend a fence she'd thought irrevocably broken.

As she followed her mum through the narrow hallway, she inhaled deeply, the familiar aroma of baked golden syrup and rolled oats from her mum's signature Anzac biscuits filling the air, enveloping her in its warmth, assaulting her senses with vivid memories of juggling a hot biscuit from hand to hand before cramming the delicious crunchy goodness into her young mouth.

Her throat clogged at the memory, and she swiped a hand over her eyes, only to be confronted with more memories as she dropped her hand and her misty gaze alighted on the old corkboard next to the fridge, bearing old Christmas cards she'd made at primary school, her first finger-painting, her old high-school year photos.

'Nothing's changed,' she murmured, her gaze sweeping over the dresser covered in imitation Wedgewood plates, the windows draped in faded gingham, the ancient Aga stove and the worn wooden table with its four spindly-legged chairs.

'Not much does around here.'

Her mum bustled about the kitchen as she always did, though rather than plonking her favourite chipped enamel teapot on the table, she carefully placed her good china one down, the teapot she'd only ever used for 'fancy' guests.

Right then it hit her. She'd become a guest in

her own home—the place she'd grown up, the place she'd always felt safe, the place where she'd first dreamed of a life far, far away.

'Don't stand around, love. Tea's getting cold.'

Just like that, the tears started, a tiny trickle which soon became a cascading waterfall, while great sobs racked her body as she collapsed into her mum's open arms.

'There, there, love. This has been a long time coming. Let it all out.'

She did, crying bucket-loads for the lost years while her mum rubbed her back in small, soothing circles as she had when she'd broken her arm jumping off the shed roof as a kid.

After what seemed like an eternity, her sobs petered out, and she pulled away, dashing a hand across her stinging eyes.

'I'm sorry, Mum.'

'Don't worry, love. Nothing a good cry can't fix.'

'But it's been so long…' She trailed off, her throat clogged with emotion at the depth of love she glimpsed in her mum's eyes.

'We knew you'd come back eventually.'

Patting her shoulder, her mum picked up the

teapot and filled china cups to brimming, adding a dash of lemon to hers, just as she used to.

'I wasn't going to, you know.'

Her mum's hand stilled, and the teapot wobbled before she carefully placed it on a coaster. 'Then what changed your mind?'

'Blane. He's back in my life. And he said some things about the past that got me thinking.'

Picking up her tea, she took a sip, savouring the strong tannin mingling with the tart lemon. She hadn't had tea since she'd left here, deliberately turning her back on her roots, desperate to shrug off a past that had dragged her down. Or so she'd thought.

'Go on.'

Her mum offered her a plate of Anzac biscuits, and she shook her head.

'I need to say this, to get it off my chest. I've spent a lot of years resenting you and Dad for not supporting my dreams of moving to Melbourne, for manipulating me.'

Sipping at her tea, she forced herself to raise her gaze and meet her mother's unwavering one.

'I blamed you for holding me back, thinking

you were control freaks for doing what you did. But it took Blane's objectivity to make me realise perhaps you did it out of love. That I was your only child; maybe you wanted to hold on too tight.'

Taking a deep breath, she ploughed on. 'Guess you didn't understand that I loved you both so much that even after I'd left town I would've always visited. I wouldn't have forgotten you.'

Reaching over, she grabbed her mum's hand and squeezed tight. 'Leaving Rainbow Creek was never about escaping you. You and Dad were great parents. I just wished I'd told you that the night we had our big row rather than saying half the things we said. I'm sorry.'

Tears shimmered in her mum's eyes, and, with a shock, she realised she'd never seen her mum cry. Not once.

In all the years growing up, her mum had been incredibly strong: working manic hours at the coffee shop, always putting a decent meal on the table, helping out at the school, never complaining about her workload.

How had she repaid her? By blaming her for something that wasn't entirely her fault.

'We're the ones who owe you an apology.'

Taking a tissue out of the gigantic pocket on the front of her apron, her mum blew her nose loudly before continuing. 'You're right. I was a control freak. I didn't want you to leave, so I manipulated the money situation. What you don't know is why…'

Her mum trailed off, looking older, frailer than she'd ever seen her. Raising stricken blue eyes to hers, she continued. 'I was like you once. Pie-in-the-sky dreams of the big city; I couldn't wait to escape my mum's clutches. But, unlike you, I was stupid enough to run away to Melbourne with barely a cent to my name. I fell for the first guy who looked my way and ended up pregnant—and alone when I told him.'

Camryn's sharp intake of breath hissed dramatically through the kitchen as she looked, really looked, at the woman she thought she'd known all these years.

'I told my mum, and she didn't want a bar of me, wanted to teach me a lesson; then I miscarried, also alone, and it was the worst experience of my life.'

As if the pea-soup fog that occasionally blanketed Rainbow Creek in the winter had lifted the blurred edges from her eyes, she suddenly saw everything in crystal-clear clarity.

'That's why Nan left all her money to me. And why you didn't want me to go to Melbourne on my own. That's it, isn't it?'

She didn't need her mother's mute nod to confirm what she already knew. It had never been about her folks trying to hold her back. It had been about two parents being protective, willing to do whatever it took to hang on to their only child.

'Your father wanted you to have the money when you turned eighteen, but I didn't. He doesn't know about my past. He doesn't know that the reason it took so long before I was ready to start a family was because of the miscarriage and the hash I made of my life back then. And I wanted to shield you from all that, to hold on to you for as long as I could. I was stupid and selfish, and I'm sorry, love. For everything.'

Shaking her head, she enveloped her mum in a hug. 'We made a right mess of things.'

'That we did, love.'

Feeling as if a ten-tonne weight had lifted off her shoulders, she pulled back, smiling for the first time in ages. 'You do know this means I'm not moving back. But I plan on not being a stranger.'

Raising her cup of tea in her direction, her mum chuckled. 'You're always welcome. You always have been. This is your home.'

Home.

Why did that word conjure up visions of a huge house perched on a cliff, a house filled with precious, all-too-brief memories of a man she could never forget?

'You were right about Blane, too. If he's back in your life, he obviously was true to his word when he told us back then that he'd always love you, that he was only leaving for your own good.'

Camryn blinked, wondering if she'd heard correctly. Her mum had only ever criticised Blane, from the first moment she'd brought him home.

'Why didn't you tell me you'd spoken to him, that he'd said that?'

Not that it would have changed anything back then. She'd been so young, so idealistic, and she'd had so much anger against the guy who'd captured her heart before breaking it. Hearing he'd left for her own good would have merely exacerbated her fury at being ditched.

Her mum frowned, and her lips puckered in the disapproving 'prune face' she remembered from the rare detention note she'd brought home.

'Because I'd already blurted out the truth about the money in that God-awful argument, and you wouldn't have believed anything else I had to say.'

Her mum's lips compressed further. 'I made so many mistakes. I should've told you the truth a long time ago.'

She smiled, raising her teacup and gently clinking it with her mum's.

'Here's to burying the past, digging up the future, living in the here and now.'

At the tinkle of fine china touching, she knew that was exactly what she had to do, tell Blane the truth, no matter how much her heart ached at the enormity of it.

CHAPTER ELEVEN

BLANE strode along the riverbank, whistling an old Eagles tune and scanning the dappled shadows for Cam.

The Rainbow Creek Motel hadn't been anything like Hotel California, but what it lacked in ambience it more than made up for with its functional rooms, which enabled the two of them to lose themselves in each other's arms all night.

It had been incredible. It was as if stepping back in time to where they'd first met had helped them reconnect on so many levels.

'Hey, you.'

Her soft voice startled him as she popped out from behind a towering eucalypt, her French braid unravelling, her olive top blending with the bush surrounds.

'Hey, yourself.'

He reached out to her, taking her hands in his, caressing the backs of them before raising a hand to trace the contours of her beautiful face.

'I have to admit, you were very mysterious about having me meet you down here, but now that we're here…' He glanced around, the tranquillity of the sluggish river bubbling over flat-bed rocks, the buzz of lazy dragonflies and the far-off caw of a magpie beckoned like a peaceful oasis. 'I think you're a genius. It's very secluded, perfect for—'

'Ssh.'

She planted a swift, scorching kiss on his lips, the kind of kiss to give a guy very firm ideas of what he'd like to do with his wife in all this isolated bushland.

However, before he could deepen the kiss, she broke away, her mouth twisting in a grimace, the devastation in her eyes scaring the hell out of him.

'What's wrong?'

He reached out for her, but she held up her hands to ward him off as a strange sense of foreboding stole through him.

She hadn't asked him down here to indulge in

a bit of afternoon delight. Far from it, if her rigid back, clenched fists and clamped lips were any indication.

Tugging on the end of her plait, she slowly raised her eyes to meet his, wide and beseeching and clouded with agony.

'I need to make you understand,' she said, her voice soft and tremulous.

'Understand what?'

'Why I'm doing this. Why we can't be together. Why—'

'Hold on a minute and back up. What do you mean we can't be together?'

He couldn't comprehend it let alone believe it. One moment they were planning to move into the house at Barwon Heads in a few weeks, the next she was ending it?

'I can't give you what you want,' she blurted, her anguish audible. 'I've seen the way you are with your nieces and nephews. I know how much you want kids, no matter how much you say I'll be enough for you. And after that night in the hospital, I know I can't go through any more procedures. I've been through too much already, and I can't face any more…' Her words petered out as she sank onto a nearby log, dropping her head in her hands.

'We don't have to go down that route. We can adopt. We can—'

'No.'

Her head snapped up, her eyes bleak. 'I'm going away. To Europe. It's something I've wanted to do for a while, and I think now is a good time.'

She was running away, just like he had years earlier.

Maybe she was scared of how fast this had all happened, maybe she didn't fully trust him yet, but she was running nonetheless.

'I think you're using the kids issue as an excuse,' he said, rubbing the back of his neck till it hurt. 'But if you need to go away, take some time to think things through, go ahead.'

'I don't need to do any more thinking.'

Her almost whisper had him dropping to his haunches to hear her, to be near her, to reach out and touch her in a world dangerously close to spiralling out of his control.

'Don't do this, Cam.'

He touched her leg, his heart sinking when she flinched away.

'I have to. It's the only way.'

She'd tugged so much on her plait it had unravelled, and her hair fell forward, shielding her face from him. But he didn't need to see her expression. He could hear how much she was hurting, could see it in the defeated slump of her body.

'Why are you really doing this?'

He had to ask, had to get answers to the questions swirling around his brain, no matter how much he wouldn't like her response. 'I need to know.'

Slowly, painfully, she lifted her head, pushing her hair back with a shaky hand. 'I can't be the wife you want me to be.'

'Can't or won't?'

She shook her head, trying to hide the shimmer of tears, but he'd already seen them, already felt them like a kick in the guts.

'I'm going away so you can get on with your life.'

He wouldn't give up on them, not when every

word she uttered, every anguished line of her body told him she didn't want to do this.

'You are my life, Cam. It's as simple as that.'

Bundling her into his arms, he didn't let go, not when she stiffened, not when she tried to push him away. Instead, he cradled her close, gently shushing as the tears tumbled down her cheeks and drenched his T-shirt, rocking her back and forth until her sobs subsided.

When she'd finally quietened, he leaned back, tilting her face up.

'I'm not a fool. I know you don't trust me enough to believe me when I say kids aren't an issue as long as I have you. I know you're pushing me away out of some misplaced idea that I'll be happier that way. But I won't be, not unless you're with me.'

His jaw jutted, as if challenging her to argue with him. He expected it, would take great delight in shooting down each and every crazy argument she threw his way.

To his surprise, her face softened. 'Want to know why I brought you here?'

He didn't need her to tell him. He remembered

every twig, every rock, every leaf of this place. It was where they'd first made love, where he'd asked her to marry him.

It was a special place, *their* place, a place made for magic, a place where anything could happen.

'Tell me,' he said, slowly strumming her back, knowing every dip and curve intimately.

The small smile he'd glimpsed playing about her mouth while she'd darted a glance around the riverbank vanished.

'Because this is the place it all started. And this is where it has to end.'

'Cam—'

'No, let me finish.'

She placed her palm against his lips, dropping it quickly when he kissed it. 'I believed you when you came back into my life and told me why you'd walked out on us. You said you'd put my dreams ahead of your own. Well, I'm returning the favour.'

'But that's crazy! My dream is you.'

She shook her head, her bereft expression cutting straight to his heart and cleaving it in two.

'I'm just a part of it. Your dream is for a family,

a family as great as your own, a family filled with kids and love and laughter, and I want that for you. I want it for you so badly.'

Clutching at his T-shirt, she hauled him close, her face mere millimetres from his.

'I love you. I've always loved you, and that's why I have to do this. I need you to understand. I need you to let me go.'

He didn't have time to respond. She crushed her lips to his in a shattering, heart-rending kiss that reached down to his very soul, leaving him yearning and devastated and vowing he'd never let her go no matter what.

Wrenching her mouth away, she hugged him close, burying her face in the crook of his neck, nuzzling him like she'd done many times before.

'Take your trip, take as long as you like, but know this, Cam. I can't let you go. I'm going to fight for us, for as long as it takes.'

He sensed her smile against his skin and wanted to leap up and swing her around in victory. Instead, he held her upper arms and set her back from him.

'That's right. Do what you have to do. But when you get back, I'm going to be waiting for you.'

Cupping his cheek, she murmured, 'You need to follow your dream.'

'I am.'

He didn't know how long they stayed like that, hungry gazes locked, hers stubborn, his hopeful, and as the sun set over Rainbow Creek, he hoped that when she took this trip, she wasn't taking his hopes and dreams for the future with her.

CHAPTER TWELVE

CAMRYN strolled over the ancient footbridges in Venice, she sighed over dusk in Paris from the top of the Eiffel Tower, she marvelled at the British architecture along Oxford and Regent Streets, but it wasn't until she reached Rome that the futility of what she was doing struck with a vengeance.

She'd deliberately distanced herself from Blane for three months, hoping her actions would speak louder than her words.

He hadn't believed her when she'd said they were over. He wouldn't accept her returning the favour he once did her, so she'd done the only thing possible and stayed away despite every cell of her body straining to board the first flight back to Melbourne after his first call. And his second.

It had shattered her completely to ignore his

attempts at contact, but she'd had to do it in the hope he'd move on. And now?

Looking around, watching a handsome Italian man in a designer suit strolling hand in hand with his equally gorgeous girlfriend across the piazza, she knew this wasn't enough.

Beautiful cities steeped in culture had acted as a suitable distraction for a while, but no amount of statues and paintings by the masters or concerts by virtuosos could eradicate the great, gaping hole in her life without Blane by her side.

She'd tried, she'd really tried to do the right thing and set him free, but the thought of him waiting for her, the memory of the many times he'd told her she was enough for him, had reverberated around her head endlessly until she kept coming back to the same conclusion. She had to return home. To her husband.

Decision made, and feeling more energised than she had in months, she sipped on a deliciously frothy cappuccino, eager to return to her hotel and send Blane an email. She was going home to be with the man she loved.

Unable to keep the smile off her face, she drank

quickly, glancing at her watch and trying to figure out the time difference between Rome and Melbourne, fervently hoping he'd be up so she wouldn't have to wait too long for a reply.

However, as she finished her cappuccino, her stomach roiled unexpectedly, and she stared into her cup in disgust, wondering if the milk was off.

'*Signorina?* Is everything all right?'

Forcing a smile for the elderly waiter when in fact she wanted to make a bolt for the Ladies, she said, 'I'd love a glass of water, please.'

'*Bene!*'

Straightening his shoulders, he beamed at her, his proud smile suggesting he'd find a well and dredge up the bucket himself. 'Another cappuccino to go with it?'

'No, thanks.'

As another wave of nausea hit, she slid the cup across the table towards him. 'I've had enough, thanks.'

As he bustled away, she rubbed her tummy, hoping she hadn't picked up a bug. For a girl who lived and breathed coffee, the smell of it had never made her feel like this before.

Suddenly, she sat bolt upright, clutching at the table to steady herself as a faint buzzing filled her head, making her feel faint. Something her mum had once said…about not being able to work in Ma and Pa's when she'd been pregnant because of the smell of coffee…

She shook her head, dismissing the ludicrous thought in an instant. There was no way she could be pregnant. Well, okay, considering what she and Blane had got up to a few months ago there was the remotest chance. Her periods had been extremely light, but she'd put that down to all the air travel she'd been doing. Was it a possibility? After all, the doctors had said it would be difficult to conceive naturally, not impossible…

Nah…it couldn't be. But what if it was? A pure, indescribable joy rushed through her, making her want to leap from the table and run through the piazza with her arms outstretched and twirling like Julie Andrews in *The Sound of Music*.

She had to find a chemist and hope her meagre Italian extended to requesting a pregnancy test.

If it was true…if the unbelievable had

happened, the reunion she had planned for her husband would take on a whole new dimension.

She could hardly wait.

Blane tipped out of the hammock, stretched and glared at the laptop that had disturbed his peace. Not that it was the computer's fault. He'd been the lazy one, too damned tired to switch it off after surfing the Net for a patio set, the call of his brand-spanking-new hammock too strong to ignore.

He'd always wanted one, the type of wide, comfy sling he could lie back in and sway, obliterating the day-to-day grind.

Until now, he'd never had the opportunity to just 'do nothing', nor the space. His penthouse in Melbourne wasn't exactly a hammock kind of place.

Frowning, he glanced at the computer screen. He'd taken care of a few residual business emails earlier and had no idea who caffeine-chick@hotmail.com was, the sender of the email dropping into his inbox the offender who had disturbed his peace.

'Caffeine chick?'

As he slid his index finger over the glossy flat mouse pad, he froze. No, it couldn't be. Why would Cam be contacting him after all this time? From an email address he didn't recognise?

He scanned the unopened message for clues, but there were none. The subject line was blank, and all he had to go on was the name of the sender.

The pointer hovered over the email, curiosity urging him to open it, common sense telling him to delete it unopened.

If it was from her, he didn't want to read it, had no intention of reneging on the decision he'd made. It had taken him this long to get past the insane expectation: every time the phone had rung, he'd hoped it was her, every time the doorbell had rung, he'd willed it to be her. Crazy, seeing as she was on her overseas jaunt and had made it more than clear they were finished by ignoring every one of his attempts at contact.

She'd almost killed him that last time at Rainbow Creek, telling him she loved him but had to let him go anyway. That wasn't love, it was madness, and he'd tried everything to convince her otherwise. But she'd still left, had effectively wiped him from her life, and it still hurt. A whole damn lot.

The loud squawk of a hungry seagull swooping nearby broke into his thoughts, and he clocked to open the email in a reflex gesture, sending the gull an angry glare a moment before realising how stupid he was being. With a sardonic chuckle, he returned his attention to the screen and focused on the brief email, his gaze instantly jumping to the name on the bottom.

Cam X.

Not Camryn. Cam. The informal name she didn't let anyone use but him, most often in the throes of passion when he'd whispered her name. Cam. With a kiss.

Frowning, he tore his gaze away from that one, small, significant X and started at the beginning.

Hi, Blane,
Hope you're well. Will be home in a week. Must see you when I return. It's important. Sorry for everything. Will explain all when I get home. Keep dreaming.
Cam X

'Keep dreaming'... That was all he'd been doing for the last six years: dreaming of making something of himself for her, dreaming of offering her the world on a silver platter when they reunited, dreaming of a happy marriage with the woman he'd loved since he'd first laid eyes on her.

But she hadn't wanted a bar of his dreams. She'd left and ignored him since to prove it. So what did she mean by 'keep dreaming'? Was she over her funk and ready to believe in them, this time for keeps?

Sinking onto the canvas chair in front of the fold-out table where his laptop perched, he rested his elbows on the table and dropped his head into his hands. The urge to respond to her email was powerful. His fingers burned with it.

But he'd made a decision after that first fortnight when she'd ignored his messages. He'd give her time and space. He wouldn't do any more chasing; he'd sit back and keep the faith, knowing that the true test of their relationship to see if she loved him enough to come back was to set her free.

He couldn't waver now, no matter how much he wanted to respond.

There was too much at stake: their entire future.

Straightening, he stabbed at the delete key, obliterating the temptation to have a moment of weakness with one easy click.

He'd waited this long for her.

What was another week?

Camryn scanned her emails on a daily basis, hand trembling as she manoeuvred some dodgy mouse in the equally dodgy hotels she stayed in for the next seven days before returning home, heart racing, the weight of expectation making breathing difficult, the subsequent let-down almost devastating.

Blane didn't respond. Not even a brief one-liner, not a word to hang a scrap of hope on, nothing.

Initially she'd reasoned he didn't have to respond; she hadn't asked him to. However, as the days dwindled along with her hopes, no amount of positive self-talk in the world could erase the gut-wrenching truth: she'd achieved her objective. He'd moved on with his life.

Dubai, Hong Kong, Singapore flashed by in a kaleidoscope of bright lights, monstrous malls and skyscrapers, but nothing, not even a dazzling display of fabulous shoes in the biggest shoe shop in the world, could lighten her heart.

She trudged through the final leg of her trip, her spirits limping into Tullamarine airport on a foggy Melbourne morning, the familiar city skyline doing little to ease the permanent ache deep in her soul. Heading to the Niche would have been her first instinct, but she couldn't face it, not today.

Valentine's Day.

The worst day of the year had rolled around again, and, while Blane hadn't responded, she couldn't help but wish he'd remember today and what it entailed. The anniversary of their first meeting. The anniversary of the night he'd walked back into her life and changed it for the better.

Sighing, she hefted her suitcase off the carousel, popped up the handle and pulled it behind her, heading for the taxi rank. No, she couldn't face the Niche today. Time enough to face the future…tomorrow.

* * *

Blane hadn't been back to the Docklands for over four months. He'd avoided the place, missing Cam too much, preferring to conduct the few meetings with the builders at the house or at his apartment.

However, Dirk had insisted he needed a caffeine fix at his favourite café, and he'd caved, knowing it wouldn't be long until Cam returned and he'd have his answers then. It would be a quick meeting, their last, as the house had finally reached lock-up stage.

Reaching the café, he stopped dead, his gaze riveted to the banner bearing corny cherubs strung across the front windows.

Valentine's Day.

Hell, he'd forgotten. In the blink of an eye he was transported back to a year ago when he'd strolled into this place and taken a chance on love again. Now, if only his wayward wife could take a chance on him…

Slamming his hand against the enormous glass door, he pushed it open and headed for the furthest table away from the cooing couples. Dirk hadn't arrived yet, leaving him with too much time on his hands—too much time to look around, too much time to remember...

'Hey, Blane. Long time no see. Though it's pretty obvious why you haven't been in, what with the boss lady traipsing around the world and all. What'll it be?'

Glancing up, he smiled at Anna, momentarily blinded by her garish, orange, pink and purple kaftan.

'And if you say a pair of sunglasses, I'll spit in your coffee.'

He winced. 'Sorry. Am I that easy to read?'

Anna propped her ample hip against a nearby stool and sighed. 'No. I've had that same look from everyone in this place today. No one appreciates a good fashion statement these days.'

'I'll take your word for it.'

He knew jack about fashion. Apart from the fact he loved Cam's usual café outfit of tight jeans, knee-high black boots and clingy bright pink top. She made a statement all right, and, despite his vow to play things cool, he couldn't help but look around in the vain hope she'd come strutting in here with her funky plait over one shoulder and that sassy gleam in her eyes.

'You miss her, don't you?'

Understatement of the year, he thought as he sat back and ran a hand over the back of his neck.

'It's been too long.'

'She's crazy about you, you know. Never seen her so happy.'

Jerking her thumb towards the banner, she said, 'Maybe this fat guy with the bow and arrow has more talent than I give him credit for.'

Had he made Cam happy? Truly happy? The type of happiness she'd do anything to preserve and nurture and build upon?

'She came home this morning but won't make it in here today.' Anna paused, tapping her gnawed pencil against the pad in her other hand. 'Not unless she has good reason to, and maybe I'm looking at him.'

'She's home?'

His nonchalant act flew out the window at the news he'd been waiting for, and it took all his willpower to sit there and act casually rather than race up to her apartment.

'I'll bring you an espresso, and you can think about it. But I gotta warn you, the chubby cherub's in a romantic kind of mood today, and Valentine's Day guarantees happy endings for everyone. No use fighting it.'

A happy ending for him and Cam? He wished. Then again, since when had he relied on wishes? He made things happen. He went out there, grabbed what he wanted, thrived on a challenge. He'd done it his whole life, first in the construction world, now with resurrecting his marriage.

So what was stopping him from making things happen with Cam? He'd stepped back, just as she'd asked, but what if playing it cool had been the wrong tactic?

What if he should have pursued her to the ends of the earth to prove how much he loved her?

He found his gaze drawn to the banner again, where Cupid seemed to be smiling down on him with an arrow aimed in his direction.

'Go ahead, shoot,' he muttered, glancing at the happy couples around him, drawn by the intimate smiles, the touches, the murmured sweet nothings, wanting what they had so badly.

He sat bolt upright, stunned by the simplicity of it all. He had a plan. A good one. And just like the blueprints for his house, he had to start at the ground level and build upwards, putting each step in place before he could achieve the best result.

'Here you go.'

Anna placed a steaming espresso in front of him, a pierced eyebrow raised. 'Well? Are you going to make Cam's day or not?'

'Actually, I've been thinking about that…'

Crooking his finger, he waited till Anna leaned forward before divulging some of his plan and the part she had to play in it.

CHAPTER THIRTEEN

CAMRYN had just stepped out of the shower and towel-dried her hair when her mobile rang.

Staring at the display screen, her heart sank. It was the café, which had closed an hour ago, meaning the alarm—linked to her phone—was playing up again. Anna had mentioned it had been a problem while she was away.

Great. Looked like her plan to head on over to Blane's straight after her jetlag-induced all-day nap and pick-me-up shower had hit a snag.

She loved the Niche, adored every chic inch, from the silk bolster cushions to the exposed beams and everything in between, but it was times like this where being her own boss wasn't the be-all and end-all she'd once thought.

Dragging on her favourite purple yoga pants and matching striped hoodie, she slipped her feet into fuchsia flip-flops, grabbed her keys and headed to the café.

The buzz of Melbourne at night hit her as she stepped out of her apartment building and crossed the road to the café, and a thrill of pleasure shot through her.

This was why she'd moved here in the first place: the neon-lit restaurants, the bars packed to capacity with revellers spilling out onto the sidewalk, the glittering cityscape backdrop reflecting off the water.

Oh, yeah, Melbourne was where it was at…but was it where *she* was at these days? That all depended on one very sexy husband…

Shaking her head, she unlocked the rear door and slipped into the café, waiting for the beep of the alarm and, predictably, greeted by silence.

'Useless piece of…'

She froze, the hair on the back of her neck standing on end as she saw a silhouette rise from one of the sofas in the lounge area and turn towards her.

Adrenalin shot through her as she cast a desperate glance at the set of cake knives several metres away. Several long metres away, and as the shadow moved towards her, she stood paralysed, belatedly remembering the spate of robberies eleven months ago when she'd moved in with Blane, her heart in her mouth and her pulse hammering at a frightening pace, until she recognised who the intruder was. Sagging with relief against the bar, she took great gulps of air to fill her constricted lungs.

'What are you doing here? You scared me half to death!'

Blane smiled, and her lungs didn't let up. If anything, they seized more.

'Sorry. I wanted to surprise you.'

'Well, you certainly did that.'

His smile faded, and she realised how aggressive she sounded, softening her voice as she stepped out from behind the bar towards him. 'Actually, it's good to see you. I'm glad you're here.'

'Are you?'

He scanned her face, searching for answers she had every intention of giving him.

'When you didn't answer my email, I thought you might've m-moved on.'

She couldn't even say the words, let alone think them.

'I was giving you the space you needed.'

'Oh. So now—'

'That was then. This is now.'

Reaching out, he drew her to him gently, as if expecting a rebuff, when all she wanted to do was fling herself into his arms and hope he'd never let go.

'I have so much to say to you,' she murmured, her heart thumping at the hope in his eyes, forcing her to look away, only to focus on his lips instead.

'There's plenty of time to get to all that.'

Anticipation buzzed through her veins as the lips she found infinitely fascinating drifted towards her, promising the future she hoped they'd have once he heard her out.

However, talk was the furthest thing from her mind as his lips brushed hers, once, twice, before crushing hers in a passionate, mind-blowing kiss, effectively obliterating everything but this moment, this man.

Pyrotechnics exploded in her head as he

deepened the kiss, rockets and sparklers and pin-wheels of sensation ricocheting through her, his tongue teasing hers, his hands everywhere, exploring, touching, caressing, driving, wild need pounding through her till she could barely stand. She clung to him, in desperate need of an anchor in a world turned topsy-turvy when she least expected it.

She'd dreamed of him, of this kind of kiss, all through Europe, had harboured a secret yearning that her trip would miraculously change things for them, and she'd come back ready to take a chance on for ever. Well, it looked like she'd got both her wishes, though right now the kiss was taking over everything.

But it couldn't. She had too much to say to him.

On a soft sigh, she broke the kiss, burying her face in the crook of his neck and inhaling deeply, his subtle cedar scent filling her, soothing her weary soul.

'So, I guess we should get around to having that chat,' he said, smoothing her hair in a rhythmic, lulling motion that had her snuggling into him further. 'Hey! You cut your hair.'

He pulled back, running his fingers through her chopped, layered locks, a bemused expression on his face.

'Took you long enough to notice.'

Her mock frown didn't last as he rubbed several strands between his fingertips, the sexy glint in his eyes telling her he approved of her new look.

'It looks great.' He captured her face, his thumbs brushing her cheekbones, his tender expression conveying more than words ever could. 'You look great.'

She could say the same about him, but she'd never been one for understatement. He looked sensational, from the top of his wind-ruffled brown hair to the soles of his well-worn sneakers. After spending months in Paris, Rome, Milan and Venice, she'd seen lots of hot guys in designer duds, but not one of those well-dressed, smooth European men could hold a candle to the guy who made denim and a cotton T-shirt look like *haute couture*.

Capturing his hands, she tugged them down, his touch creating havoc when she needed her wits about her.

'Come on. I really have to say some stuff before I burst.'

Wariness flickered in his eyes, and he grabbed her hand as if fearing she'd flee.

'I'm not going anywhere.' She squeezed his hand as she slid onto the nearest bar stool and patted the one beside her.

'Does that mean now or ever?'

'That depends on you.'

To her surprise he released her hand, propping against the bar rather than taking a seat, his serious expression sending her nerves into overdrive.

'You know how I feel, but I'm not going to push you anymore. You've had your time away. You've done what you had to do. And I'm still here. But this is it, Cam. I love you, but I'm not going to spend my life waiting around for someone who doesn't love me enough in return. So why don't you tell me what you're thinking?'

Fair enough, but where did she start? She wasn't prepared for this. In Europe, she'd mentally rehearsed this exact scenario a million times, yet, now that her little problem with a faulty alarm had turned into a golden opportunity with the man she loved, she was lost for words!

Reaching up to tug on her plait, she came up empty, and that was when it hit her. She'd start with the hair, and the rest would follow.

'I had a hair cut in Rome. Exactly twenty minutes after I had an epiphany.'

He didn't say a word, and his raised eyebrow conveyed scepticism rather than interest in what she had to say.

'I was sitting in a piazza, having coffee, knowing it was all wrong without you there. The whole trip was wrong without you to share it with.'

He frowned, confusion clouding his handsome face. 'But I thought that's what you wanted?'

'I did. At least, I thought I did. I was so caught up in returning the favour you did me that I lost sight of one salient fact. Your dream is my dream, too.'

'So what are you saying? You want to try and have a baby?'

Her mouth twitched. 'Actually, it's too late for that.'

Silence. A long, drawn-out, tension-filled

silence broken by the slight hum of the cake fridge and the sharp crack of ice from the freezer.

Okay, so she'd kind of rushed the most important part of her speech, but now it was out there she needed reassurance. Heck, she needed him to bundle her back into his arms and say it was the best news he'd ever had, and that they'd spend the rest of their lives together.

'Are you saying—'

'I'm pregnant!'

His grey eyes widened with shock as he ran a hand over his smooth jaw, an almost comical look on his face when he distractedly realised he'd shaved rather than sporting the stubble she adored.

'Pregnant? But…but…'

'Pretty amazing, huh?'

He didn't move. Not a muscle, not a twinge, and fear rocketed through her that she'd pushed him away so far there was no coming back.

'I don't believe it.'

He opened and closed his mouth several times, doing a fair goldfish impression, before a slow smile spread across his face. 'We're going to have a baby.'

'We sure are.'

She hopped off the bar stool and stood there, shuffling from one foot to another, impatient for him to sweep her into his arms and tell her this was the start of the happily ever after he'd always wanted.

Instead, he just stood there, his goofy grin fading, replaced by a wary glint in his eyes.

'This is why you came back. Not because you want me or this marriage so badly you can taste it, but out of obligation.'

'No!'

Bunching his T-shirt in her fists, she shook him, willing him to believe her when she hadn't done much to inspire it lately.

'I came back for you, only you. It's always been you. The baby is a bonus, an amazing, precious miracle, but I'd already made up my mind to come back before I discovered I was pregnant.'

She relaxed her hands, splaying her palms against his chest, feeling the rock-steady beat of his heart, never surer that she wanted to feel it for the rest of her life.

'I love you, Blane. No more trips. No more

putting your dreams ahead of mine. This time it's going to be *our* dreams all the way. That's what I want. What about you?'

After an eternity, his expression softened and he covered her hands with his, gently prying them loose before intertwining his fingers with one of them.

'Come on. I'll show you what I want.'

Taut with tension, her nerves strung tighter than Cupid's bow, she fell into step beside him, somewhat reassured by the fact he was holding her hand while terrified he hadn't actually spelled out what he wanted yet.

'Where are you taking…'

The rest of her question died on her lips as he led her around the corner into the private lounge area of the café and she caught sight of her favourite part of the Niche decked out in countless tea-lights casting dancing shadows against the mauve walls.

'How did you do this?'

'Anna.'

He led her forward, and she gasped as she caught sight of her favourite pink champagne truffles, imported from an exquisite chocolatier in the UK, laid out on a silver platter, next to a matching silver bucket with a bottle of chilled Dom Perignon champagne waiting to be opened. Brushing a kiss against her lips, he hit the play button on the sound system remote, and the crooning sounds of 'Fly Me to the Moon' filled the air, her starry-eyed gaze locking with his, her heart expanding with love.

'Why did you do this?'

Drawing her down onto a sofa, he reached behind a bolster cushion and handed her a small square box. Her heart stuttered, her pulse pounded, and her brain refused to compute the implications of what could be inside such a delicate, tiny box.

'I think you'll find your explanation in there.'

Raising wide eyes to his, she fumbled the box, catching it before it landed in the truffles, all thumbs when it came to untying the thin silver ribbon and flipping open the top. Her breath caught as she nudged the top open and peered inside, disappointment ricocheting through her as she poked the silver key chain with a miniature coffee cup dangling from it, the heady premature elation of a moment ago dissipating in an instant.

'It's a key chain.'

Her voice sounded flat, and she dragged her gaze to meet his, confused by the sparkle in his eyes.

Taking the box from her, he opened the palm of her hand and slid the key chain into it before closing her fingers over it.

'Ah…but it's not just any key chain. It goes with this.'

He reached behind another cushion and produced a flat, slim parcel wrapped in indigo embossed paper, tied with more fancy silver string.

'If this is some weird Valentine's Day thing—'

'Just open it.'

He pushed the parcel towards her, and she had no option but to place the key ring on the table and open her next surprise, more than a little confused when the wrapping fell away to reveal a map.

'Maybe I'm still jetlagged, but I'm not getting this,' she said, raising an eyebrow as the corners of his mouth twitched.

Easy for him to laugh; she'd just unburdened her soul a few minutes ago hoping for the same from him, and all she'd got were a few bizarre presents.

Taking the map out of her hands, he unfolded it, laid it on the coffee table, and smoothed it flat.

'Here. This should make things a lot clearer.'

He pointed to a large red X in the heart of Melbourne. 'The café is here.'

'Hmm, much clearer…not.'

Her brows knit in concentration as she followed his finger as he traced a major arterial to another red X.

'Barwon Heads is here.'

'Yeah…'

A glimmer of hope had her clenching her hands to stop from reaching out for the map and rattling it in his face, urging him to get to the point.

'It's approximately eighty-five minutes between here and there. Short enough to commute if someone wanted to have the best of both worlds. A little sea change mingled with a healthy dose of city life, perhaps?'

The tiny bud of joy in her heart unfurled and blossomed as she pushed aside the map and flung herself into his arms, her loud 'woo-hoo' reverberating around the empty café.

'I take it this means you like the idea?'

His confident grin had her whacking his chest in a playful slap.

'You had this planned all along? Even before I told you how I felt?'

'Sure did. Cool, huh?'

'But what made you change your mind? You ignored my email.'

The mere thought of what she'd gone through, the pain she'd endured when he hadn't responded, cast a momentary shadow on her happiness. She never wanted to go through anything remotely like it again.

They belonged together. For ever.

She'd make sure of it, if it took a thousand compromises and a million kilometres on the clock of the car she had to buy considering she'd be making daily trips between the city and the sea.

Pushing the hair back from her face, his hand lingered on her cheek, the tenderness in his gaze taking her breath away.

'It's a guy thing. I'd pushed you enough, and it hadn't worked, so I took the cool approach instead. You know, the whole "treat 'em mean, keep 'em keen" thing. And, hey, you're here and you're mine, so I guess it worked.'

She opened her mouth to promise he'd never have to play it cool with her again, but he placed a finger against her lips.

'But just so you know, that was the first and last time I let you walk away from me.'

Resting his forehead against hers, he murmured, 'This is it, Cam. We belong together. For the long haul.'

On a ragged breath, he pulled away as she blinked back tears of joy, and slid down onto one knee.

He clasped her hand, his earnest expression tugging at her overflowing heart.

'My beautiful, headstrong, independent Cam, will you marry me, again? Will you commute in sickness and in health? Will you fill that nursery nook with our babies, however many we're blessed with, and stay by my side for as long as we both shall live?'

'I will,' she said on a whisper, tears sliding unchecked down her cheeks as he pushed another box into her hand, though this time he did the honours of opening it.

She'd never had a ring first time around, had never been a jewellery type of girl, yet the minute she laid eyes on the exquisite diamond solitaire, she fell in love with it and, with shaking hands, tried to take it out of the box.

'Here. Let me.'

With love blazing from his eyes, he slid the ring onto her third finger, raising her hand to his lips, where he proceeded to kiss every knuckle, every fingertip of her trembling hand while she stared in open-mouthed shock at the man of her dreams and the ring which signified she'd agreed to be his wife, for good this time.

'Not having second thoughts already?'

Snapping her mouth shut, she ducked her head and planted a swift, reassuring kiss on his lips, tempted to linger longer…like a lifetime.

'I've never been surer of anything in my life.' She locked gazes with him, satisfied to see nothing but quiet confidence in his. 'As for you pulling out all the stops tonight, you know I'm not a romantic kind of girl, right?'

'Yeah, right…'

With a slow, sexy grin, he plucked a truffle off

the platter and waved it in front of her, brushing it across her lips in the barest of touches, tempting her to taste it, seducing her with his smouldering stare.

'You know I think Valentine's Day is a crock.'

She groaned as he half popped the truffle into his mouth, leaned forward and offered the other half to her, his lips touching hers as she bit into the rich, succulent sweetness, savouring the searing touch of his lips as much as the burst of delicious goodness.

'So you said.'

His fingertip traced her bottom lip, picking up traces of sugar while her bones melted and her brain fogged and desire churned deep within.

'But you want to hear something funny?'

'I'm not in the mood for jokes. I'm in the mood for something else entirely.'

He leaned forward and touched his mouth to hers, licking the sugar from her lips, tasting better than any truffle she'd ever had.

'I'll tell you anyway,' she whispered against the corner of his mouth, her head falling back as his lips slid across her jaw and down her neck.

'Maybe I was wrong. Maybe the chubby little guy with the bow and arrow knows a thing or two about this romance business. After all, we did meet on Valentine's Day. And you did walk back into my life a year ago on Valentine's Day. And here we are, a year later, happily married and pregnant on Valentine's Day. Are you sensing a pattern?'

He smiled and cradled her close. 'Happy anniversary, sweetheart, the first of many more,' he murmured, a second before his lips closed over hers, sealing their incredible, fatalistic union with a kiss.

As Camryn's eyes fluttered shut, she caught a glimpse of Cupid on the banner strung over the door, sure the wink she saw must have been caused by a wind draft…or a figment of her deliriously happy imagination…or the matchmaking cherub having a laugh at her expense.